livia squealed and gave Ivy a huge hug. 'We g
be twins on screen! This is amazing.'

'But, Olivia,' Ivy protested. 'I can't act. I'
ppier behind the camera.'

'So, why haven't you told Harker this?' Oli
a ked.

'I tried, but he wouldn't listen.' Ivy sighed.
ne truth is, if I'm not in the movie, then you
v n't be either. Harker insists it's the two of us
c nothing.'

Sink your fangs into these:

🦇

Switched

Fangtastic!

Revamped!

Vampalicious

Take Two

Love Bites

Lucky Break

🦇

Sienna Mercer

MY SISTER THE VAMPIRE

STAR STYLE

EGMONT

With special thanks to Sara O'Connor

For Mom and Dad, just in case

EGMONT
We bring stories to life

My Sister the Vampire: Star Style first published in Great Britain 2011
by Egmont UK Limited
239 Kensington High Street
London W8 6SA

Copyright © Working Partners Ltd 2011
Created by Working Partners Limited, London WC1X 9HH

ISBN 978 1 4052 5700 8

1 3 5 7 9 10 8 6 4 2

A CIP catalogue record for this title is available from the British Library

Typeset by Avon DataSet Ltd, Bidford on Avon, Warwickshire
Printed and bound in Great Britain by the CPI Group

Chapter One

I'm not dreaming, Olivia Abbott thought. She ran her fingers over the layers of pink chiffon that stretched out from her waist as she sat in the back of the limousine with her sister. The rhinestones on her pink peep-toe shoes winked at her.

On the other side of the black dividing screen was a chauffeur with white gloves. There was enough room for ten back here, but her bio-dad, and chaperone for the evening, was sitting up front to let them have some privacy. Olivia was on her way to the biggest event of her whole life.

It was like a fairy tale come true – without the wicked stepsisters.

'This is so much fun,' she squealed to her twin sister, who was sitting across from her, flipping through the song playlists on the limo's custom sound system.

Ivy Vega tilted her head to the side, making the black chopsticks holding back her dark hair look like the hands of a clock. 'You mean, you enjoy wearing beautiful dresses and driving in cars through crowds of paparazzi all desperate to know who you are? How strange!'

Olivia stuck her tongue out. 'The dresses, definitely. The car, a little bit, but the photographers . . . not so much,' she replied. She didn't want crazed cameramen following her every move; she just wanted to see the first movie she'd ever been in. 'The main thing is the movie!'

A few months ago, Olivia had won a small

part in *The Groves*, which starred the two biggest Hollywood actors on the planet: Jackson Caulfield and Jessica Phelps – and this Saturday night was the movie's nationwide premiere right here in Franklin Grove.

'My sister, the movie star.' Ivy leaned forwards, holding out her hand like she had a pad of paper. 'May I have your autograph?'

Olivia gave an exaggerated toss of her hair and put her nose in the air. 'I don't *do* autographs.'

Then the two sisters burst into giggles.

Olivia couldn't imagine anyone ever wanting her autograph. *Things like that just don't happen to normal girls like me*, she thought. It still felt a little unreal that she was going to walk down a red carpet.

'Now let's see what goodies we've got in here.' Ivy lifted a leather armrest, revealing a bottle of sparkling punch and a bowl of cherries. Lifting the bottle out of the built-in chiller, Ivy pointed out the label advertising the film. 'They don't miss an opportunity for promotion,' she said wryly.

Since the announcement that *The Groves* would be fast-tracked through production to make a spring release, Franklin Grove had been inundated with advertisements. Even Olivia was beginning to tire of the posters that adorned every billboard and shop window in town with Jackson and Jessica's smiling faces.

She looked out of the tinted window to see clusters of people under the streetlights holding up handwritten signs and trying to peer into the cars. The advertising had clearly worked because everyone seemed near hysteria. The limo was two blocks from Franklin Grove's Picturedrome, where the premiere was taking place, but the car could only creep forwards because of all the crowds.

'Jack-son, Jack-son, Jack-son,' chanted a group of four girls clustered on the sidewalk wearing matching cowboy boots, just like the ones Jackson wore.

Olivia's heart thumped a little quicker. After an embarrassing introduction a few months ago, Jackson Caulfield, mega-star, had actually become her boyfriend. Just thinking about it made her swoon a little. She was dating the biggest teen star on the planet! But it was a total secret to the outside world.

Jackson's manager, Amy Teller, had decided that it would upset Jackson's fans if he had a girlfriend, so the two of them still hadn't gone public. It wasn't the biggest secret in Olivia's life – *that* was the whole vampires-are-real thing she'd learned when she found out about Ivy's dietary requirements. But keeping her romance quiet meant that she couldn't be seen with Jackson as anything other than a friend and fellow actor. Hard, when all she wanted to do was kiss him!

She looked across the limo at her sister, who was wearing a goth-gorgeous black Chinese dress with red dragons embroidered over it. They looked like complete opposites, but that was just going to make it more fun to walk down the red carpet together. If she couldn't walk down with Jackson, Ivy was the next best partner.

'You certainly look ready for your debut,' Ivy said. 'That dress is amazing.'

'Thanks,' Olivia replied. 'But you mean: *our* red carpet debut. You're coming with me!'

'No way!' Ivy leaned back into her seat. 'I'm putting a jacket over my head and sneaking in the side entrance. Besides, the two of us together would look like a fairy princess and her evil stepmother.'

'Come on, Ivy!' Olivia protested. 'I know

you don't like the fuss, but people really won't be watching *us*. They're all waiting for Jessica and Jackson.'

The limo crept around the corner and suddenly the dark sky was lit up by spotlights, camera flashes and a huge neon sign announcing the premiere of *The Groves*.

'Pardon me,' came the driver's posh voice over the car's speakers. 'We shall be arriving shortly.'

Ivy shook her head. 'All this glitz and glamour is not my style. This is one twin request too far,' she said, avoiding Olivia's eye. 'Sorry, sis.'

'Wait a minute,' Olivia said. 'You have dressed up as a cheerleader for me. You have worn pink, auditioned for a movie and giggled like your life depended on it for me – why is this any worse?'

Ivy bit her bottom lip.

'There's something you aren't telling me.' Olivia raised her eyebrows, waiting.

Ivy leaned forwards and whispered, 'I was sworn to secrecy.'

Olivia started to worry. Her sister never kept secrets from her; this had to be big!

'Jackson,' Ivy began, '*is* going to walk down the red carpet with you, but it was meant to be a surprise.'

Olivia's hands flew to her face. 'Really?' He must have argued with his manager, or he might not have told her about his plans. What about his fans? And the paparazzi? Still, she couldn't stop herself from bouncing a little in her seat with excitement.

'Really,' Ivy confirmed, smiling.

Olivia smiled back, pushing the worries aside. All that didn't matter. She was going to walk down the red carpet with her boyfriend. No more pretending!

'I can't wait,' Olivia whispered back.

Just then, the limo took a sudden turn, sending Olivia and Ivy sliding into the side of the car.

'Woah,' said Ivy, her chopsticks clicking against the window.

'Is that supposed to happen?' Olivia wondered, as they drove away from the movie theatre.

The black partition that separated the driver from the passengers slid down. Her bio-dad, Mr Vega, looked dashing in his full tuxedo. 'Sorry, girls,' he said. 'Change of plan.'

'Ch-change?' Olivia stammered. Now that she'd found out what Jackson was planning, she didn't want anything to change.

The driver, still keeping his eyes on the road, said, 'I'm sorry, Miss, but we've just had word that Jessica Phelps is mysteriously late. The premiere is being delayed.'

Olivia groaned. Jessica always used her celebrity status to its full potential. She had a diva tantrum on her first day of filming and demanded all sorts of special treatment. Because she was the star of the movie, the show simply would not go on without her – and she knew it.

'Don't worry, Olivia,' Mr Vega said, a sympathetic look on his pale face. 'The Food-Mart is just next door, and the production team has decided to use it as a place for all the stars to wait.'

'OK,' Olivia said weakly as the partition went back up. But really she wanted to say, 'Arg!'

'We're not exactly dressed for grocery shopping,' Ivy said with a smile.

Olivia imagined all the actors and their assistants, plus the stressed-out event pro-duction crew running up and down the aisles of Franklin Grove's biggest grocery store in their formal wear.

'It's going to be completely chaotic,' Olivia

replied. 'Jessica must be up to something.'

'We can always sneak downstairs if it gets too crazy in the store,' Ivy said.

Underneath the regular FoodMart was the BloodMart, where any vamp who was anyone in Franklin Grove went to stock up on all their midnight snacks. Biting people was so last century. You had to know the secret password to get in but Olivia was one of the few humans who had been initiated into the vampire world because she was Ivy's twin.

'Unless it's busy down there, too,' Olivia replied. She remembered the first time she'd gone into the BloodMart. It was just after she'd learned the vampire secret and she had been pretty freaked out by it all. But really, the worst she'd seen anyone get up to down there was a round of chess.

'Don't worry,' Ivy said. 'Most vamps will be

lining the streets with the bunnies to see Jessica Phelps. They'll want to see their vamp-diva in her full glory.' If only the world knew that one of their Hollywood A-listers was a vampire who filed the points of her teeth! Most people didn't believe vampires really existed – or know that normal human beings were jokingly called 'bunnies' by the vampire community.

As they pulled into the parking lot of the FoodMart, Olivia sighed. She hoped Jessica Phelps hadn't ruined her chance to walk down the red carpet with her boyfriend.

The FoodMart was jammed with people, like a crowd at a hanging.

Do they really need all these people to just walk down a carpet? Ivy thought.

Under the glaring fluorescent lights, she, Olivia and Mr Vega fought their way past the bread section to the baby aisle, where it looked like there was some space.

'Excuse me!' Ivy said to a burly man clad in black who was blocking her way.

He was on his phone and didn't hear her. 'Red fox underground,' he was muttering. 'Underground!'

'Hey!' said Ivy, poking him with her elbow.

Burly Man peered down at her and then grunted, shifting the tiniest fraction so she could squeeze by.

'What is going on?' Olivia wondered, carefully holding up the train of her dress so it wouldn't get stepped on.

Ivy looked around. She couldn't even guess. She only recognised half of the people as movie crew from her time as an extra on the set. Who were all the others? Just as she passed the diaper shelf, she came face-to-face with

Sophia Hewitt, her best friend.

'What are *you* doing here?' they asked each other at the same time.

Sophia was wearing a long-sleeved black mini-dress and black-and-white striped pantyhose. Her camera was at the ready in her hands.

'There's some mysterious, end-of-the-world delay with our female star, and we all have to wait here for her to be ready,' Olivia explained.

'And I have to say,' Mr Vega put in, 'that it all seems a little unorganised.'

Sophia chuckled and spread her hands to indicate the supermarket. 'Here lies the answer.'

'Here?' said Olivia, looking around at the pastel-packaged baby milk.

'Well, underneath here,' Sophia said.

The only thing underneath the FoodMart was . . . of course! The BloodMart.

'That is so rude!' Ivy declared.

'What is?' asked Olivia, clearly baffled.

'Jessica must have decided she needed a snack from the Blood Mart before facing the cameras,' Ivy growled, realising that the people she didn't recognise would be the ones following Jessica around. There was a girl in head-to-toe pink 'JP' merchandise and two heavyset men with sunglasses hovering nearby. 'She's made hundreds of people wait so she can grab a Vampish Delight or something.'

Sophia nodded. 'I've been assigned to her press entourage by *VAMP* magazine and she decided halfway to the Picturedrome that she simply had to stop for a snack. She's downstairs now, browsing like she has all the time in the world.'

'You're on official magazine business?' Mr Vega asked, looking impressed.

Ivy knew that Sophia had made friends with Georgia Huntingdon, editor of the most popular fashion magazine in the vampire world, earlier this year when the twins were on the cover.

'I'm the new Franklin Grove photo correspondent,' Sophia said with a proud smile.

'Killer,' Ivy said.

'With all the celebs in town, it's keeping me very busy,' she said, snapping a photo of Ivy and Olivia.

'Stop it!' Ivy said, batting away the camera gently, but Sophia just grinned.

'You two were in the movie, and you look fantastic. If it gets me a photo credit in *VAMP*, I'm gonna go for it!' She snapped a second photo, ignoring Ivy's protests.

'You were in the movie just as much as me,' Ivy said. They had been extras in one of the diner scenes – along with the unbearable Charlotte Brown.

'Yeah, but I'm not the sister of the newest

up-and-coming star,' Sophia said, winking at Olivia, but she wasn't paying attention.

'Sophia, have you seen Jackson? Is he here, too?' Olivia was wringing her hands.

Sophia nodded. 'I think he was by the vegetables when I walked past a few minutes ago,' she said.

Ivy hoped Jessica's little food mission hadn't messed up Jackson's plans for the red carpet. She thought it was high time that her sister could stop hiding in the shadows.

'Thanks.' Olivia turned to Mr Vega. 'Can I go find him?'

'Sure, honey,' he replied. 'Just find me before you head out of here.'

The crowd was starting to thin a little, as Olivia slipped away. Near the butcher's counter, Ivy saw a short man with his back to her, waving his arms angrily in front of an assistant wearing headphones.

'. . . think she can do this! *Non, non*!' he was saying in a heavy French accent.

Ivy guessed right away who it was: Philippe, the director of the movie. She knew from her time as an extra that no one did grumpy like he did, and he must be livid about Jessica's little detour.

'Think I should try for a picture?' Sophia said.

'If you want to get your hand bitten off,' Ivy replied. 'He looks worse than usual.'

'Ivy! Sophia!' A trim woman in a tailored black pantsuit waved at them from in front of the fish display.

'It's Lillian,' Sophia said, waving back.

'Come on.' Ivy grabbed her dad's hand and pulled him over. 'Dad, this is Lillian Margolis. She was the assistant director on *The Groves*.'

'Second assistant director, actually,' Lillian said, extending her slender hand. She was wearing a simple but elegant silver bracelet. Her usually messy black hair had been tamed into a classy bun, held back by a pretty onyx hair clip. She looked like Audrey Heppingburn in the classic vampire flick *Breakfast of Tiffanies*.

'How do you do?' Mr Vega asked, with a little bow. Two pink spots appeared on his usually pale cheeks as he took Lillian's hand in his. 'A pleasure to meet you,' he murmured. 'Please call me Charles.'

'Charles,' she said gracefully, smiling a little. 'Lovely to meet you, too.'

She gave Ivy and Sophia each a hug then turned back to Mr Vega. 'You have two very talented daughters, Charles. I hope Olivia enjoys the final product tonight.'

'Oh, I'm sure we all will,' Mr Vega replied, smiling. 'Uh . . . How long have you been in the movie business?'

'That's dangerously close to asking a lady her age.' Lillian waggled her finger at him, pretending to tell him off.

'No, no,' Mr Vega looked sheepish. 'I meant –'

Lillian cut him off cheerfully. 'Let's say that I've worked on fifteen films and counting. And what do you do?'

'He's an interior designer,' Ivy boasted. 'If you like things dark and velvet, he's your guy.'

'Really?' Lillian raised her eyebrows. 'My home in LA actually needs refurbishing.'

'Ooh, LA!' cooed Sophia.

'I love LA,' Mr Vega said brightly, taking Ivy by surprise. He had only been there once, and with all the sunshine, it wasn't exactly a vamp-friendly place.

Lillian smiled at Mr Vega's eagerness, while Ivy had to double check that her father hadn't been taken over by aliens: pale skin, not green

. . . check. Two eyes not five . . . check. Still a vampire, not an alien. But her dad was acting excited. Well, as excited as her super-composed father ever got.

'Maybe you could all come and visit my home in Hollywood and we could talk about some ideas?' Lillian asked.

Mr Vega bowed slightly. 'I would be happy to, as long as you think my taste will complement yours.'

'Well –' Lillian leaned in closer, like she was about to share a secret. 'Like you, I have special . . . culinary requirements of the red-meat variety.'

'You mean, you're . . .' Ivy trailed off, not wanting to say anything that might break the First Law of the Night. No humans could ever find out about vampires' existence and, since it was so hard to tell who was and who wasn't, it was always tricky when you met someone you didn't know but suspected might be.

'I'm rather partial to Marshmallow Platelets,' Lillian said with a grin.

Ivy grinned back. *Cool,* she thought.

'I think there are some drinks on a table over by the refrigerated aisles,' Mr Vega said, suddenly as enthusiastic as he had been when he was pretending to enjoy visiting Mister Smoothie a few weeks ago – but this time it felt genuine. 'Can I get you a drink, Lillian?'

'I'll come with you,' she replied and the two of them walked off, chatting about arrangements for a spontaneous trip.

'Oh my darkness,' said Sophia. 'We're going to Hollywood!'

Ivy grinned. She couldn't wait. 'This totally sucks.'

Chapter Two

The FoodMart was much emptier now.

Burly Man from before bustled past. 'I'm chasing the rabbit down the hole,' he said into his phone.

'That is the lamest code-speak ever,' Ivy said. But at least Jessica's entourage had followed her downstairs so there was a little breathing room.

'Let's find Olivia, so we can tell her about going to Hollywood,' Ivy said, leading Sophia through the refrigerated section.

'Hey,' said an unshaven older guy wearing a Harker Films T-shirt, looking straight at Ivy. He flashed a big grin as he walked past. 'You were pretty good.'

Ivy stopped short. 'Who was that?' she asked Sophia. 'And what did he mean?'

Sophia looked amused. 'I don't know, but I bet Brendan won't like guys like him smiling at you like that.'

Then an older lady with greying hair, holding a clipboard, gave her a smile. 'Sweetie, you were great! Congratulations.'

Ivy was completely baffled. She couldn't let this go, so she turned and hurried after Clipboard Woman. 'I'm sorry, but what do you mean?'

'The movie, sweetie.' She patted Ivy's arm. 'Most of the crew have already seen the full screening. I bet you loved dumping that jug of juice on Jackson's head.'

'Oh . . .' Ivy said, realising that they had mistaken her for Olivia, who played a goth in the film. She decided it would be too complicated to explain. 'Thanks! It was fun!' she said brightly.

'Maybe you and Olivia should be a double act?' Sophia suggested as they walked down the soda aisle.

'Not a chance,' Ivy replied. 'I'll leave the star turns to her and stick to making things happen behind the scenes.'

'Like me!' Sophia said, holding up her digital camera. 'I'd better go find the Phelps-inator in case she's doing something particularly headline grabbing with the Platelet Porridge.' Sophia gave Ivy a hug. 'See you on the carpet!'

'But I'm not –' Ivy began but Sophia had already disappeared. 'Going on the carpet.'

'You're not?' said an unfamiliar voice behind her.

Ivy turned to see a man with shaggy black hair and a pale complexion. He wore scruffy jeans with a black blazer over a T-shirt from a band that had broken up at least twenty years ago. *He must be one of the paparazzi in Jessica's entourage*, Ivy decided.

'Nope,' Ivy said, definitively.

'But you're all dressed up, man,' he pointed out, sounding like a hippie from the sixties. Ivy guessed he couldn't be part of Jessica's flock of vampire sheep with that kind of slang. He probably wasn't even a vampire, she decided, and didn't have a clue about what went on downstairs. 'Why don't you want to?'

'Honestly?' Ivy asked, not sure why he would be asking.

'Yeah.' The shaggy-haired guy nodded.

'I think it's all a little bit dumb,' she confessed. 'All the stress, the running around and shouting. Has no one realised, this is only a movie?'

Shaggy Guy crossed his arms, grinning. 'When

you put it like that, man, it does sound kinda over the top.'

Ivy was just getting started. 'Think about it,' she challenged him. 'If they would put all the money from this premiere into a fund for graduates to go to film school – or even for underprivileged kids to go and see this movie – it would be money better spent.'

Shaggy Guy laughed. 'You've got your head screwed on, man. That's not a bad idea.' Then he walked off.

That was weird, Ivy thought, *but it seems like this movie business makes everyone a little crazy.*

🦇   🦇   🦇

Olivia felt like Cinderella, frantically searching for her pumpkin carriage before the clock struck midnight – except that instead of running from a palace, she was charging past shelves of pickles and ketchup.

'Olivia!'

She turned and saw her prince, looking charming in a black tuxedo with silk lapels. His usually wild blond hair was slicked back and his bright blue eyes were twinkling.

'Jackson,' she said, trying not to grin like an idiot. 'I've been looking for you everywhere.'

'Which is probably why you haven't found me, because I've been looking for you ever since I heard your chauffeur dropped you off.' He gathered her up in a big hug. 'You look amazing,' he whispered into her ear.

Olivia felt like she could float down the red carpet.

'Are you nervous?' he asked.

She thought about it for a moment. 'It's just walking,' Olivia replied. 'How hard can it be?'

Jackson chuckled. 'Just walking?' He pretended to be shocked. *'Just walking!* Look, Miss Up-and-

Coming-Movie-Star, there is walking and there is Red Carpet Walking.'

Olivia giggled.

Jackson put one hand on his hip. 'I will demonstrate.'

He half-strutted up the aisle, past the rows of salad dressings, with his shoulders back and his pearly whites on show. He stopped occasionally to pose and half-turn, as if imaginary cameras were flashing all around him. He walked back to her, really hamming it up.

'That looks easy enough,' Olivia said.

'I still think you should have a practice run,' Jackson advised.

Olivia smiled, tossed her hair and set off striding past the relishes. But when she stopped to do a half-turn like Jackson did, her skirt caught under her shoe and she staggered straight towards a neat stack of soup cans.

'Eek!' Olivia squealed.

Jackson grabbed her just before she knocked the pyramid of tins flying. A store assistant who was tidying up the mayonnaise at the end of the aisle shot her a dirty look.

'Oh no,' Olivia whispered. 'Why didn't I think to practise walking?'

Jackson put his arm around her. 'I think I might have a solution to your problem. What if . . .' he said with a twinkle in his eye, 'you had someone to guide you? Someone by your side to give you confidence and help you with when to stop and pose?'

Olivia realised what he was doing. He was building up to telling her that he wanted to go public and that they could walk down the red carpet together. Her heart started thumping – not quite like when they had their first kiss, but close to it. She readied herself to pretend to be surprised. *Don't grin. Don't look surprised too early.*

She could see the anticipation on his face. He was just as excited about this as she was. 'Olivia,' he said, beaming. 'I want to go public and walk down the red carpet with you!'

'What?' screeched a demanding voice. 'You can't do that!'

Now Olivia didn't have to pretend to be surprised. Amy Teller was poking her head around the corner, and she'd clearly been listening to everything they had been saying.

She strode over, her five-inch-high heels clicking along the linoleum floor. Her red hair was pulled back in a severe ponytail and she was wearing an off-the-shoulder calf-length dress made from silver satin. She looked beautiful but fierce, and ready to take charge on the red carpet for her client. She had a phone in one hand and a takeaway cup of coffee from the Meat and Greet.

'Jackson, Olivia.' She sighed. 'We have discussed this. We agreed that you would walk by yourself or with your mother or sister. And since none of your relations are here . . .'

Jackson shook his head. 'No, Amy,' he said softly. 'You talked about this, and you agreed with yourself. I want to walk down the red carpet with my beautiful girlfriend.'

Olivia wanted to do a cheer. Jackson was standing up for her – and he thought she was beautiful!

'I don't want to have to pretend to be single any more. We've kept things quiet for long enough, but we are certain about how we feel.' Jackson grabbed Olivia's hand and she thought she might turn into jelly. 'Now we want to celebrate being together – and this is the perfect way to do it. I want to be a normal teenage boy, with a normal teenage girlfriend.'

Olivia could see the store assistant hovering around the pickles, trying to listen to their conversation, but she didn't care.

'You are not normal.' Amy pointed at him, her sleek silver phone flashing under the fluorescent lights of the supermarket and her coffee threatening to spill over the flimsy plastic lid. 'You are a mega-star with millions of fans who think that you are available. If you go out there as a couple, it could end your career!'

Jackson squeezed Olivia's hand. 'If that happens, so be it.'

Olivia couldn't believe that he would be willing to give up everything for her. 'You shouldn't –'

'I want to,' he cut her off.

'Well, then.' Amy turned to Olivia with a cool stare. 'What about you? Are you ready to be universally hated by girls everywhere for stealing Jackson away?'

'Uh –' Olivia hadn't thought about that.

'There will be threads online called We Hate Olivia Abbott and groups scrutinising every little thing you wear.' Amy was leaning closer and closer. 'They won't leave you alone until there's a break up – and being in the spotlight is one of the quickest ways to make that happen. Are you sure you can handle this?'

Olivia gulped. *I can handle the existence of vampires, but what about the wrath of an army of haters?* Olivia remembered how crazy Jackson's fans were at his book signing in February.

Jackson looked at her, his eyebrows creased. 'I don't want to put you through anything horrible,' he said.

She paused for a moment, but knew she didn't want to pretend any more. 'And I don't want to date in secret any more,' Olivia replied. 'Amy, I think you're overreacting and I won't be scared into staying silent because of a few unhappy people.'

Jackson's face broke into a huge grin.

'We'll deal with it, if and when it happens,' she finished.

Amy did not look happy. She stared at Olivia, but Olivia refused to back down. She stared right back. The sounds of the hubbub going on in the supermarket around them faded away.

Amy opened her mouth, about to speak, when the shrill of her phone made Olivia flinch. It made Amy jump too, her arm jerked up and the lid of the coffee cup slipped off.

Then several things happened at once.

The froth of the coffee sloshed towards Olivia.

She tried to step away and stumbled.

Jackson started to pull her backwards.

But it was too late. With scalding heat, the coffee splashed right down the delicately layered folds of Olivia's dress.

'Oh, my goodness,' Amy gushed. 'I'm so sorry!'

Olivia looked down at the brown mess that was spreading in a stain across the beautiful pink chiffon. Her gorgeous dress; the biggest night of her life! And now it was ruined. She tried to hold back her tears.

'How could you do that?' Jackson demanded, grabbing the paper napkin out of Amy's hand and dabbing at Olivia's ruined skirt.

'It was an accident,' Amy insisted, holding up her hands. 'I didn't mean to.'

Olivia knew it was the truth but it still stung that Amy had got her way.

'There's no way I can walk down the red carpet like this,' Olivia said. 'It's over.'

Just then, a young man with a goatee and a clipboard rushed over. 'We are go. We are go. Jessica has arrived. Jackson, you're up *now*.'

'We have to get moving,' Amy said to Jackson and Olivia wished she could disappear.

'Wait –' protested Jackson. His blue eyes looked pained.

'No, go,' Olivia said. 'You can't miss your moment.'

'I don't want to go without you,' he insisted.

'You have to,' she whispered.

'Are you sure?'

Olivia didn't trust herself to speak again, so she nodded.

She watched Jackson being escorted away down the aisle with a horrified, apologetic look on his face.

My fairy tale has shattered, she thought miserably.

🦇   🦇   🦇

Ivy stepped around a display bin of multi-coloured sponges.

Wham! Someone ran straight into her — a person-sized flamingo-coloured blur.

'Hey,' Ivy started. 'Watch where you're ... Olivia?'

The pink blur was her twin sister. And she was crying.

Ivy grabbed her by both shoulders, forcing her to stop. 'What happened?'

'My dress!' Olivia spread out her dress to reveal a big upside-down u-shaped brown stain.

'Oh no!' Ivy gasped. While pastels weren't her thing, her sister's outfit was amazing. Or had been amazing.

'And Jackson's been summoned to walk the carpet.' Olivia sniffled. 'Alone.'

Ivy didn't say another word and just wrapped her arms around her sister in a hug.

'Thanks,' Olivia said, pulling back. 'I'm going to see if I can wash it off or something, so that I don't miss the whole premiere.'

'Do you want me to come?' Ivy offered, knowing how upset Olivia must be about missing her chance to go public with Jackson.

'No, don't worry,' Olivia said. 'You go find our dad and make sure he's not lost in the pet food aisle, wondering what's happening.'

Ivy nodded. 'See you inside?' Even though Ivy wasn't going to do the grand entrance, she and Olivia had arranged to sit together in the cinema. Olivia wanted Ivy there for moral support.

As Olivia nodded and hurried away, Ivy started marching up and down the supermarket aisles, looking for her dad. Just in front of the rows of checkouts, she spotted Jackson and Amy, hovering by the door, with a crew member peering at his watch.

Jackson waved her over. 'Have you seen your sister?' He tried to step towards Ivy but Amy was blocking his path back into the store.

'I saw her; she's a little upset,' Ivy admitted.

'I should go . . .' he started but Amy cut him off.

'Jackson, she'll be fine.' Amy kept looking through the big glass doors. 'We need to go any second now.'

Just then, the Shaggy Guy from the soda aisle strolled up with two young men in ties following him.

Amy's face broke into a big smile and she nudged the guy in the blue tie out of the way to approach Shaggy Guy. 'Helloooooo, Jacob. So lovely to see you!' They air-kissed.

Why does Amy care about some paparazzi man who is chasing Jessica around? Ivy wondered.

'Hey,' she said, when he glanced her way.

Amy gasped and Jackson's jaw dropped.

'Hey?' Amy said. 'Mr Harker is the head of the studio. You don't just "Hey" the person who made this movie!'

Whoops! Ivy thought. *How can this guy be the head of a studio? He looks like he needs help getting dressed in the morning.* Ivy tried to smile without looking too awkward. 'Uh . . .'

'Amy, don't be so establishment,' he scoffed, whipping out a smart phone and starting to type on it. The young man that Amy pushed out of the way rolled his eyes.

Uh oh, Ivy thought. *An anti-establishment man of Hollywood? I'm not even sure if that's possible.* Everything was just getting weirder and weirder.

'I've already met this young star, and I like her attitude.' His shaggy hair flopped around as he nodded enthusiastically.

Ivy blinked. *Star?*

Amy's eyes almost popped out of her head.

'She could be huge, man,' said Mr Harker.

'What do you mean?' Ivy spluttered.

Jackson gave her a nudge, smiling. 'Ivy and Olivia, taking the world by storm.'

'Who's Olivia?' Harker asked.

'She's the goth neighbour in the movie, and Ivy here is her twin,' Jackson explained. 'And Ivy was an extra in the diner scene.'

'Hey, now I see,' Harker said. 'You guys are twins.'

Ivy nodded, biting her lip to stop from saying, *Duh*.

'Dude, your sister was good,' Harker went on. 'Really good.'

'Yes, she is,' Jackson put in, and Amy shot him a warning look. Ivy guessed that Amy didn't want Harker getting the hint that Olivia and Jackson were dating.

Harker turned to Ivy. 'Are you ready?'

'For what?' Ivy had no idea what was coming next. This was turning out to be the strangest supermarket experience of her life.

'For your walk down the red carpet, man?' He leaned in close. 'You and your sister are gonna be the next big actresses to hit Hollywood – and I'm going to be the one who discovered you.'

Mr Harker ushered Amy, Jackson and Ivy towards the door. 'It's a shame your sister isn't here,' he said. 'But you and Jackson are coming out with me.'

Ivy couldn't believe that the head of a Hollywood studio wanted her to be an actress. Every cell in her vampire body was telling her to flee. This was the exact opposite of how she'd wanted her evening to go.

Ivy stopped next to the enormous display of brooms that was by the front doors. 'Look, this really isn't my scene.'

'Of course it's not,' Mr Harker said. 'That's exactly why you're perfect for it. Now, come on!'

The Blue Tie guy nudged her in the back. 'You can't say no to Mr Harker,' he said.

Ivy gulped and stepped out into the night. From across the parking lot, she could see flashes of light and hear crowds screaming. It was like a horde of demons ready to swallow her up.

Olivia was reading the label on the back of a bottle of detergent for delicates, wondering if it would work on chiffon, when she heard, 'Darling, what a dress!'

She looked up to see a man in a purple silk suit with an open black shirt underneath. He was clapping his hands together in appreciation at her dress. Olivia remembered him from the set of *The Groves*. He was Spencer, the flamboyant make-up artist.

He leaned in closer. 'Don't tell anyone I said this, but your dress beats Jessica's in the class category any day.' Olivia blushed. 'But what are you doing hiding back here, when they're calling everyone out for the carpet cues?'

Olivia turned to show the full hideous stain, holding out the draped folds of the skirt panels for him to see.

'Oh, no, no, no!' he tutted, backing away in shock.

'Coffee,' she told him.

'It's worse, honey,' he retorted. '*That* is not any coffee. That is a soy latte with . . .' He sniffed the air. 'Vanilla syrup.'

Olivia put the bottle of detergent back on the shelf and plopped down on to the cold floor. 'I can't go out there looking like this.'

'You are absolutely right, you can't!' He grabbed her hand, pulled her to her feet and dragged her down the cleaning aisle.

'What —?' Olivia started. It felt like her arm was about to pop out of its socket.

'Trust me,' Spencer replied as they turned a corner. Olivia had to scoot around a store assistant who was restacking the candy bar section at the end of the aisle.

He finally stopped in the homewares section and selected a pair of big orange scissors. He slapped a 20 dollar note on the shelf and ripped open the packet.

'Wait, I —' What was he planning to do with those?

'Sshh!' he said abruptly.

'But —' Olivia started.

'Sshh!' He held up a finger. 'Your dress is ruined. Nothing will get that stain out. The premiere has started and you are about to miss your red-carpet debut. Let me fix this.'

Olivia bit her lip as Spencer knelt down and began to cut. The store assistant peered down the aisle at them and Olivia hoped that he wouldn't try to have them arrested for the scissors.

She smiled brightly and waved at him.

The assistant grunted and went back to his CocoLoco bars.

With what seemed like only six snips, Spencer had removed the stained area of the skirt, leaving a C-shaped curve at Olivia's right leg. The edge of the curve had been cut into jagged sections, just like teeth marks. *It looks like a shark has taken a bite out of my dress!* The white chiffon underneath was on show and . . . and . . .

'Well?' he said.

'I look OK,' Olivia said, amazed.

'OK?' Spencer gasped. 'Honey, this is divine. Everyone will love it.'

Olivia wasn't entirely sure but she was so

grateful to Spencer for trying to help. 'You're right!' She put on her bravest face. 'Divine.' She flashed a smile and pretended the homewares aisle was the red carpet. She strutted down a few steps, paused, turned and strode back with not a single stumble.

The store assistant was staring again, so she gave him a little wave.

'Great walking, sweetie, but what's the pose?' Spencer asked.

'The pose?' Olivia was focusing on getting the walk right. Now she had to do a pose, too?

'Look,' Spencer said, grabbing her shoulders and looking her right in the eye. 'You are going to have to show off this fabulous dress, and you can't just hope the photographers get a good shot of you – you have to make it happen!' Spencer did three quick poses in a row: his head over his right shoulder, both hands on his hips with a pout, and one foot kicked up in the air. 'Which one did you like best?'

'Um . . .' Olivia was a little overwhelmed.

'You try.' Spencer commanded.

Olivia put one hand on her hip, turned to the side and smiled wide.

'Not bad, but turning hides my creation! How about this?' Spencer put both hands behind his back, in an innocent pose, turned his face to one side and batted his eyelashes.

'If I don't have to do the eyelashes,' Olivia said, 'that works for me.' She struck the pose and crossed one leg in front of the other.

'Oooh, honey,' Spencer purred. 'Perfect. Now get out there and be fierce!'

'Thank you for being wonderful.' She air-kissed him and then caught herself. The Hollywood way was infectious! Olivia didn't mind, as long as it didn't get out of hand.

Now for the red carpet, Olivia thought. She knew she wouldn't be there in time to walk down the red carpet with Jackson, but she thought maybe she could find Ivy or Mr Vega lurking around.

As she rushed past the cash registers she heard someone calling her name.

'Olivia, over here!' It was her bio-dad, looking every inch the 1940s movie star next to the glamorous Lillian. They had obviously been getting to know each other.

'Oh no!' Lillian had noticed her dress.

'What happened?' Mr Vega asked.

'There was a spill.' Olivia didn't want to dwell on it. 'It's fixed now, and I'm ready to get out there and face the cameras.' Olivia still thought no one was really going to be paying attention, so as long as she could get inside the cinema and watch the movie, her night would be complete.

'That cut looks really striking,' Lillian said. 'I think it actually works.'

Olivia nodded.

'Well, then,' Mr Vega said, offering his arm. 'As your sister seems to have already gone ahead, would you do me the honour of allowing me to escort you?'

Olivia grinned. 'I would love to.'

Lillian beamed with approval. 'You two look gorgeous. Now get out there and dazzle them! I'll be right behind you.'

Olivia's heart started to pump as her heels clicked across the parking lot towards the Picturedrome. Over the crowds that were surrounding the entrance, all with their backs to her, she could see bright spotlights and flashes. There was a huge cheer and Olivia guessed that it must be because Jackson or Jessica was making their appearance.

She took a quick glance at her reflection in a window as Mr Vega led her between a van and a sports car. Her diamond choker sparkled under the parking lot lights and her brown curls fluttered gently in the breeze. There wasn't far to go now until they would be at the end of the carpet, making their appearance.

Now or never, she thought. The noises got louder and Olivia could hear people shouting out to Jessica to sign autographs.

'We love you, Jessica!' screamed a brown-haired girl.

Olivia wasn't sure whether she was relieved or disappointed to follow Jessica – either way, the crowd wouldn't be much interested in her. Jessica was in her element, greeting all her fans like they were long-lost friends.

A young man with a goatee hurried over.

'Olivia Abbott plus one?' he asked. She

nodded. 'Just a minute. Lillian, you can go whenever you want to.'

Lillian gave a knowing smile and mock-whispered, 'That means no one cares when I go!' She gave a little wave and said, 'Good luck.' She headed into the crowd and disappeared.

'I guess this is it,' Olivia said, but her father's gaze was fixed on the retreating silhouette of Lillian.

'What, honey? Oh, yes,' he said, giving her arm a squeeze. He was watching the crowd again. 'This is so exciting for you, Olivia. I'm so proud of you for following your dream and getting this part.' He pulled her into a hug.

Olivia wished her adoptive parents could have been here, too, but she was only allowed two extra tickets to the red carpet, and they'd gone to Ivy and Mr Vega.

'Thanks,' she replied. Even though she

couldn't walk down the red carpet with Jackson, she was so happy to be able to do it with her biological dad. She couldn't believe it had only been a few months since she'd found out who he was.

'Olivia, you're a go.' Mr Goatee pushed them towards the red carpet and a team of security guards materialised and stood along the crowd, forming a path.

This was like the biggest pep rally of her life.

There were young girls and parents in the crowd, photographers and journalists. There were little strobe lights chasing up and down the sides of the carpet and music from the movie's soundtrack played from big speakers. The sight of the red carpet laid out in front of her, leading up the steps into the cinema, gave her such a thrill that she didn't even have to think about putting on her smile.

This is amazing, Olivia thought.

'You look beautiful,' Mr Vega whispered. He took the first step on to the carpet and Olivia followed. She relaxed her shoulders and lifted her chin. They were approaching the press area where all the photographers were lined up to catch the arrivals.

Everyone was staring and Olivia heard one man with a grey moustache ask, 'Who is that?'

'I don't know,' said the woman in a trench coat next to him.

Olivia caught sight of Sophia, elbowing her way to the front of the crowd of photographers. Sophia gave a little wave and then said to the woman, 'That is Olivia Abbott, the next big thing.' She started snapping away furiously with her camera.

'Well, whoever she is, I love that skirt.' The woman nudged the photographer standing next to her. 'Get her.'

Suddenly, all the cameras were flashing.

'Olivia!' cried the woman. 'Do a turn!'

Mr Vega stepped back so that Olivia could have her photo alone. She took a step, turned and then struck the pose that Spencer had shown her.

'*EveryWoman* magazine wants to know who designed that dress?' called another lady wearing all black.

Olivia wasn't sure what to say. 'It's a one-off design by a friend of mine.'

'Nice friend,' came the envious reply.

It was going really well. Thanks to Sophia and Spencer, it turned out that people were interested in her after all. It felt like the most exciting moment of her life . . .

I just wish Jackson was with me, she thought wistfully.

Chapter Three

Ivy was lying on the black leather sofa like a corpse. She was wearing her long, fitted black dress with bell sleeves and a black choker and felt like sleeping for a hundred years after yesterday's fiasco. Thank goodness it was a Sunday – she didn't have to think about school for hours and hours.

'I never want to see another movie again; let alone be in one,' she said, remembering the hysteria that bombarded her as she was practically dragged down the red carpet by Amy and Mr Harker last night. Cameras flashing, all those people staring.

'Well,' replied Brendan, who was lying the opposite way, top to tail. 'I hope you mean after this one.' Brendan and Olivia were over at Ivy's to watch *The Parent Trap*. 'Because I want to see the end.'

'Ha ha,' Ivy said. The movie was paused because they were waiting for Olivia to come back from a phone call with Jackson downstairs in Ivy's bedroom.

'Seriously, though,' Brendan said, pushing his curly black hair out of his eyes. He had on a T-shirt that said Mad World. 'It should be pretty easy to avoid being in a movie.'

Ivy sighed. 'Not if you have the Hounds of Hell after you.' When Brendan raised an eyebrow Ivy explained, 'Amy Teller and the head of the studio that made *The Groves* have decided I'm the next big thing.'

'You?' Brendan said, sitting bolt upright.

'Thanks,' Ivy replied drily and closed her eyes. 'You don't have to be so surprised. But, as it happens, I agree with you. It seems the only reason I'm "it" is because I don't want to be.'

'That doesn't make much sense.' Brendan wedged himself up on to the sofa, sitting with his legs hanging over hers. Even though they had been dating for almost the whole school year now, it still made Ivy's heart race a little when he got this close.

'Because I was so super-casual at the premiere, Mr Harker has decided to put me in a movie,' Ivy explained. She reached over to the dark glass coffee table to grab her Strawberry HemoGlobules drink. 'I couldn't stop them dragging me down the carpet and they were whispering plans for the next movie over the top of my head.'

At the premiere, Ivy had told Amy that under no circumstances would she be interested in any of this acting-career nonsense. She would rather be trapped in a room with Charlotte Brown for all eternity than have a single moment of people staring at her, but Amy had just replied with an infuriating, 'No one says no to Mr Harker.'

Ivy sighed and flopped her head on to Brendan's shoulder. 'Olivia is the actress in the family, and I'm the one who likes lurking in the shadows,' she said.

'As long as you don't mind my company in the dark,' Brendan suggested.

Ivy smiled back and wriggled around to give him a hug. 'Most definitely not.'

'OK, you two lovebats, break it up!' Olivia was climbing the stairs from Ivy's basement bedroom. Even without her custom-made pink dress,

Olivia still looked gorgeous in a lavender knitted sweater with a flower burst at one shoulder.

Ivy poked her tongue out. 'Just because your boyfriend is busy on national television, it doesn't mean you have to keep me away from mine.'

Olivia looked deflated and Ivy realised her sister might be feeling a little upset about the whole not-going-public last night. 'I shouldn't have said that,' Ivy apologised, unhooking herself from Brendan. 'I was just teasing.'

'No, no,' Olivia said. 'I'm just being sensitive.'

'It won't always be like this,' Ivy said, getting up to put her arm around Olivia. 'He was so angry not to be able to walk with you.'

Olivia nodded. 'I know. He wouldn't stop saying that on the phone just now.' She sniffled and Ivy wanted to kick herself. Today was supposed to be about cheering Olivia up, not reminding her of her troubles. 'There's a post-premiere party tonight, and I'm going to see him there.'

'How about we watch the rest of the singalong?' Brendan suggested, to Ivy's relief. 'Not that I know the words or anything.'

'I already saw you mouthing along,' Ivy said, plopping back down on the couch.

Olivia snuggled down in the single black armchair and Ivy was about to un-pause the movie when the pipe-organ doorbell rang.

The three of them looked at each other. Ivy wasn't expecting anyone else to join them. Sophia was still taking photographs for *VAMP* magazine, and Camilla Edmunson, Olivia's best friend, was visiting her aunt for the weekend.

'Could one of you get that?' called Mr Vega from the kitchen. 'I'll be right there!'

Ivy hurried to the huge oak door and pulled it

open slightly, wondering if it might be a cleaning-product salesperson.

Instead, it was Lillian, looking casual-fabulous in a black turtleneck, jeans and brown ankle boots. She was carrying a foil-covered tray. 'Dessert!' she said and Ivy stepped back to let her into the wood-panelled entryway.

'Hi, Lillian!' Ivy said. 'Nice to see you again.'

'Thanks,' she said, and waved at Olivia and Brendan, who were staring from their seats. 'It's nice to see this house. I can tell I'm going to get good advice from your father.'

'Definitely,' Ivy agreed. 'But what are you doing here?'

'Your dad wanted to go over some decorating ideas ... Oh, I love that movie!' Lillian declared, having caught sight of the TV screen. 'Let's get together, yeah, yeah, yeah,' she sang.

Ivy smiled and then laughed out loud when

her dad came hurrying out of the kitchen. He was wiping his hands on the pink floral print apron that someone had given him as a joke when he had almost moved away from Franklin Grove.

'Lillian,' he said, a little breathless. 'Thanks so much for coming.'

She handed over her tray. 'As promised.'

Mr Vega beamed and it struck Ivy that he seemed a lot more excited than usual to have a lunch guest. 'Double dark chocolate cookies,' he said, peeking under the foil. The most amazing chocolate smell filled the air and Ivy had to admit that Lillian's dessert did seem worth getting excited for.

'Lunch is almost ready,' Mr Vega said. 'Ivy, will you take all our guests into the dining room?'

Ivy was surprised. She had been expecting finger foods at the kitchen counter, not a sit-down meal. 'Uh, sure. You heard him, layabouts,' she said to Olivia and Brendan, who were still lounging in front of the TV. 'Right this way,' she said to Lillian, with a little bow.

As they walked through the entryway, past the suit of armour, Lillian said, 'So, girls, how did you like last night?'

'It wasn't exactly my scene,' Ivy replied. 'But I think Olivia could get used to it.'

Olivia grinned. 'I wonder if there were any good photos of me.'

As they reached the dining room, Ivy saw that the candles were lit down the long oak table. Mr Vega was definitely out to impress. After all, it wasn't every day that a Hollywood director came to lunch.

Just as they sat down, the doorbell chimed again.

'I'll go,' Ivy volunteered, wondering who else her dad had invited over.

When she swung open the door, Sophia

hurtled inside like a whirlwind. 'We did it! We did it!' she yelled.

Before Ivy could ask what on earth was going on, Mr Vega popped his head out of the kitchen. 'Is that Sophia shouting?'

'Sorry, Mr Vega,' Sophia replied, adjusting her skull-print messenger bag. 'I hope you don't mind me barging in, but I've got some exciting news.'

'No, no,' he replied. 'Come through to the dining room. We're just having lunch.'

Sophia grabbed Ivy's hands, and bounced. Actually bounced.

'Sophia?' Ivy said warily, knowing something was up. Her friend did *not*, under any circumstances, bounce.

'I want to tell you and Olivia at the same time!' Sophia scuttled off towards the dining room, leaving Ivy to trail after.

'Ta da!' Sophia called, pulling out a stack of

magazines and waving them in the air.

'What is it?' Olivia said, standing up from her chair.

Sophia slapped each magazine down one by one: the *LA Daily*, *StarWatch*, *Hollywood Happenings*. Then she started flipping through the pages.

'There!' she declared, pointing to a spread on *The Groves* premiere with a big shot of Olivia, posing in her dress.

'Eeee!' Olivia squealed. 'It's me!'

'And me.' Sophia pushed down the page, so they could see the words in tiny type just inside the fold of the paper: 'Photo by Sophia Hewitt.'

'Olivia Abbott, supporting actress in the film, looked sharp and sparkling with her cut away dress,' Ivy read. 'Hey, that counts as a good review!'

'Congratulations!' Lillian said, clapping.

Sophia turned to the dog-eared pages in each

of the magazines. There were three other shots of Olivia, all snapped by Sophia.

'OK,' Ivy said to Sophia.

Sophia looked serious for a moment. 'OK what?'

'OK, I will forgive you – just this once – for the bouncing.' Ivy grinned and gave her best friend a hug.

Mr Vega came in, balancing six plates on his arms: burgers with fresh avocado salad and French fries, which he'd stacked up in a little tower like they were at a fancy restaurant. Ivy helped him put the plates on the table and saw that while the five vampires had pretty much rare steak, Olivia had a homemade veggie burger.

'This looks great!' Brendan said. 'I should come over for meals more often.'

'Thanks for fitting me in,' Sophia said, crunching on a pickle.

'Ketchup?' Ivy and Olivia asked at the same time.

'As if I could forget,' Mr Vega said, reaching around the door for a little tray of condiments.

Ivy covered her hunk of meat in ketchup, and Olivia dotted some delicately around her fries. Brendan dug in, but Mr Vega was still watching Lillian.

There is something going on here, Ivy thought. *Dad is acting very weird. Good weird, but definitely weird.*

She tried to catch Olivia's eye, but Olivia was still looking at the magazines. Mr Vega cleared his throat and Ivy thought he was going to say something, but then he just started eating.

Is he nervous? Ivy wondered. There was an awkward silence, so Ivy decided to fill it. 'What kind of movie are you working on next?'

'I wanted to risk doing something small on my own,' Lillian replied. 'A little independent film where I get to be full director for the first time.'

'What's it about?' Brendan asked, with his mouth full.

Lillian smiled. 'It's a documentary-drama about a dancer who was executed during World War I for being a spy.'

'Ooh,' replied Ivy. 'Sounds cool.'

'I know about her,' Mr Vega finally broke his silence. 'Mata Hari, right? She turned out to be innocent, in the end.'

'That's right,' Lillian said, clearly impressed. 'The script has gone through so many revisions, making sure we get all the history correct.'

'It sounds amazing,' Olivia said.

'Thanks!' Lillian said.

'I'm quite familiar with that time period – having lived through it myself. Perhaps I could help by reading the script?' Mr Vega offered.

Lillian laughed. 'I'm not going to reveal *my*

age, but I'd be grateful for the advice.'

Ivy watched the two adults smile at each other. When Lillian jumped up to help Mr Vega clear the plates, Ivy whispered to Olivia, 'Did you see that?'

'What?' asked Olivia.

'Them,' Ivy said.

Olivia tilted her head to one side. 'Them what?'

'Dad is acting all weird,' Ivy said.

'Because he wants to read the script?' Brendan asked, spinning around the UFO-shaped salt cellar.

'I think it's more than that,' Ivy replied. She definitely was getting a romantic vibe from the way they stared at each other. 'You didn't notice anything unusual?' she asked her sister.

Olivia was the ultimate match-maker – after all, she got Brendan to ask Ivy out on their first date. So if she wasn't seeing it, maybe it wasn't there?

'All I've noticed is that Lillian has great taste in movies,' Olivia said. 'I really like her.'

When Lillian and Mr Vega came back, carrying the chocolate cookies, with cherry sauce for Olivia and a bloody syrup for the five vampires, Ivy decided she would test her theory.

'So, Lillian.' She watched her dad as she asked blatantly, 'Are you single?'

'Ivy Vega!' Mr Vega admonished, horrified.

'Oh, I don't mind,' Lillian said, glancing at Mr Vega.

Ah ha! Ivy thought.

'As a matter of fact I am single,' Lillian said. 'This business keeps me pretty busy.'

'You don't want to date an actor then?' Ivy pressed, still looking at Mr Vega, who was leaning slightly forwards over the table, clearly listening.

'Oh no,' Lillian protested. 'They're all tans and teeth. How shallow is that?'

Ivy nodded her agreement, but caught sight of Olivia looking peculiar.

'Oh! All, apart from Jackson,' she hastily added.

Ivy bit her lip to stop the laughter that threatened to bubble up. 'So you prefer the pale look?' she went on, now cheekily grinning at her dad.

'That's enough of that,' Mr Vega said, standing up to clear some plates. 'Finish up your cookie, Miss Cross-examiner. Wasn't there going to be some homework catch-up today?'

Brendan nodded. 'I hope so, Mr Vega. I need some help with my math.' He flashed a wicked grin at Ivy. 'If you have twice as many paparazzi as celebrities and three times as many cameras as – oof!'

Ivy elbowed him in the ribs. 'This is a celebrity-free zone until I have recovered from last night,' she declared and she took her last bite of the freshly baked cookie.

'I've brought my books,' Olivia said. 'Let's go down to your room.'

The three of them carried their plates into the kitchen, and just before they went through the dining-room door, Ivy glanced over her shoulder at Mr Vega and Lillian, who were huddling close over the kitchen table, where Mr Vega had laid out some design papers.

They do make a cute couple, Ivy thought.

As they headed to the basement staircase Ivy said, 'Don't you think Dad is into Lillian?'

But before they'd even reached the bottom step, Ivy heard Lillian calling, 'Bye!' and the front door closing.

'If he was interested, I think it would be good for him to try dating again,' Olivia replied. 'But he's not doing a very good job if the second we leave them alone, Lillian flees.'

Brendan chuckled. 'Mr Vega needs to work on his game.' He pretended he was boxing, bouncing and throwing imaginary punches.

'I suppose you're the world champion, lady killer?' Ivy asked.

'There's only one lady for me,' Brendan called after her. 'And I've got her, haven't I?'

'OK you two,' Olivia said. 'It's time for math. I want to finish this so I can get home and get ready for the party tonight. My parents are going to chaperone. Ivy, I hope you're coming.'

Ivy gulped. She still hadn't mentioned to Olivia her conversation with Harker about the two of them starring in a movie together.

Anyway, it probably isn't going to happen, Ivy told herself. *Why get Olivia worked up for nothing?*

She'd had enough of all the parties, but she knew her sister wanted the moral support. 'Yes, OK, but Brendan, you have to come as my date.'

Brendan frowned. 'Sorry, Ivy, but I've got to babysit Bethany tonight. My parents are going star-gazing somewhere in the middle of nowhere.'

Ivy sighed. 'Well, at least you can help me pick out what to wear.'

'Is that Richard Redford over there?' Mrs Abbott gasped, holding a napkin full of olives pits in one hand and her silver clutch bag in the other.

'No, Mom,' Olivia said, patting her mom on the arm. 'This isn't that big a party.'

'It feels like it to me!' Mrs Abbott said. She was wearing her purple silk suit for the occasion and, with her funky lace pantyhose, she suited the glamorous party crowd.

'Isn't that Jackson?' said Mr Abbott, looking across the crowded room at someone trying to make their way over.

Olivia clapped her hands. 'Yes!' He was wearing a new black jacket over jeans and grinned as she caught his eye.

He waved her over.

'Can I?' Olivia asked her parents.

'Go, my daughter, and spread your wings,' said Mr Abbott in his typical philosophical way.

Olivia kissed him on the cheek and hurried over to her boyfriend.

'Have you met Olivia Abbott?' Jackson said to a lady wearing a blue sequined blouse. 'The most gorgeous girl here tonight?'

Olivia blushed. 'Nice to meet you,' she said, shaking the woman's hand firmly.

'Lovely earrings,' the woman said.

Olivia had chosen a green Greek tunic-style dress with large silver earrings and silver sandals. 'Thank you,' she replied. There was a mix of glamour and casual, with most of the women dressing up, with jewels and full-length dresses, and most of the men – Hollywood producers and casting agents – in tailored jackets and expensive-looking jeans.

The post-premiere party was being held in the local heritage wing of the Franklin Grove Art Museum. Mr Vega had been working for the past four months on the biggest exhibit the small museum had ever built. There were paintings and sculptures by artists from the area spanning over a hundred years. There was everything from a weathered stone gnome to an abstract painting with black splodges called 'Cemetery'.

Mr Vega had also included a section with photographs, stories and models of how the town had developed. One image showed the old railroad station, while the one next to it showed how that had become the mall.

Jackson and Olivia were standing next to a

sculpture of melted coloured glass that looked like a twisted Eiffel Tower in red, white and blue. They were each nibbling goat's cheese tartlets. There was a violin quartet playing in the corner and waitress in a tuxedo circulating with a tray.

After the woman drifted away, Jackson pulled Olivia behind the Eiffel Tower, where no one else could see them.

'I just wanted to say that I'm really sorry about last night,' Jackson said, drawing her close.

'I know,' Olivia replied. 'But it all worked out in the end.'

'We're going to sit down with Amy and decide on the perfect time to go public.' Jackson looked like he would ninja-chop anyone who tried to convince him otherwise.

She nodded. 'OK. If it's what you want.'

She leaned forwards and Jackson did, too. Just as they were about to kiss —

'There you are!' squealed a high-pitched voice. Jackson and Olivia broke apart to see Jessica Phelps poking her head around the glass tower. Jessica sashayed over and kissed Jackson on the cheek, completely ignoring Olivia. 'I've been wondering where my fabulous co-star was hiding!'

Olivia felt her face freezing into an Ivy-special death stare. Jessica was being so rude!

'Hi Jessica,' she cut in, not letting the Hollywood starlet squeeze her out of the conversation.

Jessica blinked at her, clearly annoyed that Olivia had dared to interrupt her. 'And you are?'

Olivia smiled through gritted teeth, wondering if she could get away with chucking her goat's cheese tartlet at Jessica. But Jackson stepped in.

'You remember Olivia,' Jackson said pointedly. 'She was a supporting actress in *The Groves* and is, of course, my leading lady.'

Olivia wanted to hug him again. That was the first time he'd said to anyone straight out that they were a couple. She wanted to do a cheer, she was so happy.

Jessica narrowed her eyes. 'Leading lady?'

Jackson gave Olivia another little cuddle, and Olivia smiled at Jessica.

'Well.' Jessica tossed her hair. 'How nice.' But since she made no attempt to move away and leave them in peace, Olivia could tell that she wasn't going to give up that easily. She'd obviously tracked Jackson down for a reason and Olivia had a sinking feeling that she wasn't going to like whatever it was. 'What were you two talking about?' Jessica asked.

'Well, I was going to tell Olivia about this new script I've been offered,' Jackson said. 'Amy does a little dance every time she brings it up;

she thinks it's going to be big. It's a book-to-film adaptation called *Eternal Sunset*.'

Jessica and Olivia squealed at the same time.

Olivia knew that book and the whole series like the back of her hand. It was Count Vira's most epic vampire romance and one of her favourites.

'Reading the script is the next thing on my list,' Jackson said.

'I got that script today, too!' Jessica purred, slipping her arm through Jackson's. 'I'm up for the lead. Wouldn't it be great to get Jessickson back together?' She shot Olivia a look at this point that pretty much said, 'Watch out.'

No, it would not, Olivia wanted to shout. *And the whole merged couple name 'Jessickson' sounds stupid!*

Jackson was frowning, too. 'Ah, well . . .' he trailed off.

'It would be killer if you were in that movie,'

Olivia told him, steering the conversation away from Jessica's pointed remark. 'I absolutely love those books.'

'They aren't exactly my kind of thing,' Jackson admitted.

'What do you mean?' Olivia said, hoping Jackson wasn't going to be disparaging about Count Vira's writing.

'Honestly, I'm just not a big fan of vampires,' he replied, shrugging. 'The whole idea of them is dumb.'

Jessica tossed her hair. Of course, Jackson didn't know about vampires, and it was going to have to stay that way. Olivia hated keeping such a big secret from him, but it wasn't really her secret to tell.

'Well, Jackie,' Jessica said. 'I just wanted to say that LA really misses you.' She put on a fake pout, but Jackson wasn't playing her game. He gave a polite smile, saying nothing. He'd moved to Franklin Grove to be near Olivia, and there was nothing Jessica could do about that.

'You should come back,' she purred. 'It's where you belong.' She leaned over and gave him a kiss on the cheek. 'Bye, now!' She waggled her fingers and flounced away.

Jackson looked baffled. 'She's a little over the top tonight, isn't she?'

When isn't Jessica over the top? Olivia took a deep breath. 'That's one way of putting it.'

The sign said, 'Money-crazed, desperate men abandoning all morals in the rush to strike it rich.'

Ivy sighed. *Is that the California Gold Rush or a description of the people in this room?*

She'd been busying herself reading and re-reading sections of the museum's displays to avoid having to talk to anyone. This one was about how Franklin Grove was a busy stop on the route to California.

She was keeping an eye out for Olivia, the whole reason she had come tonight, but ever since Jackson had showed up, her sister had disappeared.

A bald man to her left was flashing a chunky gold watch and designer sunglasses. A woman on her right wore a two-inch-wide ruby bracelet. The young couple in front of her had both clearly had plastic surgery.

'Oh, you're so funny!' someone declared and then burst out into a fake laugh.

Ivy didn't even have to turn around to know who it was. Jessica Phelps.

A hush fell over the crowd as an ice sculpture of Jackson's and Jessica's heads was wheeled into the room.

Jessica squealed with delight and rushed over.

'Oh, my gosh!' she practically screamed. 'It's me!'

Like we needed you to explain that, Ivy thought. *How can anyone take her seriously? She may be a vampire, but she acts like the doziest bunny there ever was.*

Ivy decided she'd had all she could take and was just about to make her way to a side entrance to sneak out when she caught sight of a familiar face. Blonde ponytail, slightly too much blusher and a little sneer. It was Charlotte Brown.

'How did she weasel her way in here?' Ivy muttered. Charlotte had only had one disastrous scene as an extra in the film, so there must have been some Daddy manoeuvring that got her an invitation.

Charlotte hovered behind Jessica, clearly eavesdropping and trying to get the starlet's attention. Ivy ducked behind a potted topiary in the shape of a peacock, so she could get closer without being seen.

When Jessica looked over, Charlotte turned on her biggest smile. 'Oh, hi, Jessica!' she said, trying to pretend that she just happened to be standing there.

Jessica raised one eyebrow.

Ivy leaned forwards and pushed away a twig that was sticking out from the peacock's tail and tickling her nose. She was hoping for a delicious cut-down. After all, Jessica wasn't nice to anyone and surely the Hollywood vamp was going to tell Charlotte to get lost.

'I just love those Bibble Bubble shoes,' Charlotte cooed. 'They must be next season's because I haven't seen them anywhere.'

Jessica looked Charlotte up and down, clearly evaluating whatever pink, fashion-victim code she was presenting, and deciding that Charlotte passed.

'You're right,' Jessica said. 'François sent them

to me straight from the prototypes.'

'Oh, you're so lucky!' Charlotte said.

Ivy let out her breath. *What a let down!* It seemed the two shallowest people currently in residence in Franklin Grove were destined to be friends. Ivy had been hoping for some kind of spontaneous combustion. Still, with two egos that size, there might be some fireworks to come.

'I love your hair, too,' Charlotte was saying. 'And your ice sculpture is so fab.'

'Thanks!' Jessica said to Charlotte. Then she narrowed her eyes. 'You must live here.'

Stop the press, Ivy thought. *The girl is a genius.*

Charlotte nodded eagerly.

'That means,' Jessica went on slyly, 'you must go to school with . . . oh, what's-her-name . . .'

'I know everyone who's anyone,' Charlotte bragged, flipping her hair.

'Dark hair, green eyes,' Jessica went on vaguely. 'Had some minor role in the movie.'

Charlotte was like a baby bird waiting for its breakfast, desperate to get the answer right. 'Um . . . oh, I know! Olivia! Olivia Abbott!'

'Hmm,' Jessica said and Ivy wanted to dump the full potted plant's worth of soil over her head.

How dare she pretend not to know Olivia's name! Ivy thought.

Ivy was just about to step out and let Jessica have it when someone tapped her on the shoulder. She whirled around to see Mr Harker wearing what looked like the same pair of scruffy jeans from last night but with a different band's T-shirt under his black blazer.

'I was hoping to run into you, man,' he said, as Ivy sheepishly stepped out from her hiding place. 'Although I'm not sure I would have expected to do it behind a manicured plant.'

Ivy offered a weak smile. *Maybe he will just decide I'm an idiot and not want me to star in any of his movies*, she hoped.

'Let's find somewhere a little more quiet to talk,' Harker commanded.

Ivy followed him through the throng to the drinks table.

'Hello, sir,' said the bartender, clearly aware who Harker was. 'What can I get you?'

'I'll have what she's having,' Harker replied and the two of them waited for Ivy to decide.

'Uh,' she stammered. 'Apple juice.'

While the bartender busied himself getting glasses, Ivy decided to be straight with Harker about her lack of acting ability. 'Look,' she said. 'I'm not really . . .'

But the sound of Jessica's forced laugh split through the crowd's murmuring and interrupted her.

'Always has to be the centre of attention,' Ivy muttered.

'That laugh is one of the most grating in Hollywood,' said Mr Harker. 'And there are some hyenas, let me tell you.'

Ivy hesitated, not sure if she should bite her tongue. After all, he cast Jessica in a movie – so maybe he didn't find her that annoying. But Ivy was never very good at keeping her mouth shut.

'Her laugh is the only thing faker than her tan,' Ivy said. 'Unless you count her hair extensions.'

Mr Harker chuckled, grabbing a stick of beef satay from a waitress's tray.

Ivy was on a roll. 'It is simply not possible to be that interested in a story about someone else's finger nails.' She sighed. 'She is obviously very good at what she does, or she wouldn't be so successful, but . . .'

'Jessica does have the looks,' Mr Harker said, but he leaned in and whispered, 'Don't you think she could do with filing her teeth more often?'

Ivy stepped back in surprise. *Only a vampire would know to say that! And that must mean he knows that I'm one, too.*

'I did a little research,' Harker explained, 'and saw the *VAMP* magazine articles on you two. You're already stars in the making, ready for the big screen,' he said.

He must have been talking about the big feature that Georgia Huntingdon did on them before Christmas, when they had just found out they were twins. And there was the one with the Queen of Transylvania.

'No, really, I –' Ivy started. *How can I tell him that a wooden stake would be better than me on screen?*

'Dude,' Mr Harker said, 'I don't want you being modest. I've already got my lawyers drafting a studio contract to send to your agent. You do have an agent, don't you?'

Ivy spotted an opportunity. 'No, no, I don't! Guess I'm just an amateur – shouldn't be let near a movie set.'

'I like your style,' Mr Harker replied. 'You negotiate your own terms. Excellent!'

Ack! Ivy thought. *What do I have to do to put him off?*

'Harker!' said a grey-haired man, grabbing a bottle of beer off the table. 'The board is all round the table, waiting for you.'

'Perfect timing, Greg,' Harker said, thumping the guy on the back. 'I've got a new star to introduce.'

Ivy gulped.

Chapter Four

'Dudes,' announced Mr Harker, 'and Dudettes.' He nodded to the three women around the table. 'You've got to meet the Next Big Thing!'

He stood aside so that everyone could get a good look. Ivy wished she could sprout bat wings and fly away.

Harker had dragged her over to a side room that opened on to the main area, where the display of the Empire State building and the Statue of Liberty was overshadowed by a round mahogany table. It was piled high with nibbles and drinks, but Ivy was too uncomfortable to get excited about the mini quiches. The sounds of the party faded as they stepped further into the room.

Now that Harker had outed himself as a vampire, Ivy could tell that all of the suits at the table were vamps and she wondered for a minute if Hollywood was run by vampires.

She hated it when people stared and the people round this table had absolutely no hesitation in evaluating her from her ponytail to her lace-up boots.

One man on the opposite side of the table put down his fork and said, 'I'm not sure about the hairstyle.'

Ivy's hands flew to her fringe. 'What?' she protested.

'The fashion is current,' commented another, like Ivy was a store mannequin.

'You know it,' Ivy retorted.

'What about the nose?' muttered a third.

'Hey, now,' Ivy started, ready to let them have it, but Harker interrupted.

'Forget all that.' He waved his hands. 'This is Ivy Vega, the edgy opposite of her *twin*, the sugar-sweet Olivia Abbott.'

'Ooooh.' That seemed to impress the group.

I'll have to tell Olivia that! Ivy thought.

'And Ivy's going to be just as good!' Harker gave a thumbs up.

Ivy was starting to get a little panicky. She needed Olivia to come and deal with all the attention.

She looked over her shoulder through the open doorway and caught sight of Olivia in the main area, practically concealed behind the glass Eiffel Tower with Jackson.

Even if I did a cheerleading routine on the table, she wouldn't notice, Ivy thought. *I'm on my own.*

'There's more,' Harker went on.

Please no, Ivy thought. She wasn't sure she could handle more.

He grinned and grabbed a leather messenger bag from under the table. 'Just this morning, I closed the deal for the option on the hottest book series in town.'

Harker pulled a hardback out of the bag and held it up. The woman closest to Ivy, in a red off-one-shoulder blouse, gasped.

Ivy recognised the book from posters in bookstores and even on billboards. It was a dark, paranormal romance called *Eternal Sunset* about an immortal vampire girl and her sister who fall in love with two reincarnated boys once a century. Totally dumb and of course it had sold a gazillion copies.

'And we need some really special actresses to play Carmina and Belinda, the two immortal vampires . . .' Ivy started to see where Harker was going. 'Carmina is a girly-girl, just like Olivia, and Belinda is edgy and dangerous, just like Ivy!'

'I should tell you –' Ivy started.

But Harker was so excited that his shaggy hair was bouncing up and down with every other word. 'Two sisters in real life, plus a great vampire actress on the big screen. What's not perfect?'

To Ivy's horror there was lots of nodding around the table.

'But a debut?' said the woman in green, sceptically. 'I'm not sure we should go with someone untested.'

Ivy wanted to kiss the woman. 'Actually, I –'

'But don't you see, Jennifer?' Harker insisted, as he leaned over the table to grab a dumpling from one of the plates. 'The wider public don't know that Olivia has a twin sister. And if we can keep it that way, we can build up a whole mystery about who we're casting. It's a publicity *dream*!'

Jennifer frowned. 'But that all falls apart the minute a pap gets a shot of the two of them together.'

Harker nodded. 'Yup, that's why I'm telling Ivy all this.' He turned to her. 'You two will have to stay on the down low.'

Don't tell everyone that I've somehow been roped in to star in a blockbuster? Ivy thought. *You'll get no argument from me there.*

'If the news gets out before then,' Harker said, 'it just won't work for the two of you.'

The gathered suits murmured like a mantra, 'Just won't work.'

Ivy started to see it clearly now.

Jennifer crossed her arms. 'That's low risk, then.' She raised an eyebrow at Ivy. 'Got that?' she said. 'If there's a news leak, your sister and you are out.'

Ivy felt like it was almost a challenge.

'What do you think, man?' Harker prompted Ivy. 'Can you do this for me?'

'Er . . .' Ivy didn't care about her film career, but she knew how much this would mean to Olivia. She'd just have to try her best at this acting game. After all, weren't there loads of actors and actresses out there who weren't exactly brimming with talent? She could be one of them! 'It's an amazing offer,' she began.

Jessica and Charlotte appeared in the open doorway, smiling brightly.

'What are you all doing, hiding back here?' Jessica said, her eyes flashing when she saw Ivy.

Charlotte piped up from behind. 'Is this girl bothering you?'

Harker didn't reply and the suits were tight-lipped. But Jessica was not about to take the hint.

Ivy realised she had the perfect opportunity to annoy Jessica. 'Actually,' she said to the group. 'I'd love to take the role.'

'Dude,' said Harker appreciatively. The suits offered a smattering of applause.

Jessica looked like her head was going to spin around in a full circle. 'What role?' she asked through gritted teeth.

'Now, now, Jessica,' Ivy replied. 'That would be a secret!'

'That's my girl,' said Harker, popping another dumpling in his mouth.

Jessica opened her mouth, then closed it. 'Well, I hope you break a leg,' she said with sickly sweet venom, and then flounced away, Charlotte trailing behind.

🦇   🦇   🦇

'There is nowhere I'd rather be than with you,' Jackson said into Olivia's ear, 'but I think Amy will kill me if I hide in this corner for the whole party.'

Olivia smiled. She didn't mind doing a circuit of the room on Jackson's arm.

As they stepped out from behind the coloured glass, Olivia caught sight of her parents chatting to another couple near the ice sculpture of Jessica and Jackson. She steered Jackson in that direction.

'Who are my parents talking to?' Olivia wanted to know.

'That's the third wife of the studio's financial guy,' Jackson whispered as they approached.

The woman barely looked older than Camilla's college-age sister and was wearing the largest diamond necklace Olivia had ever seen. 'And he's the financial guy,' Jackson added. A short, balding man was ranting about accountants.

'And I just can't tell you the headache that clause 6.83 has caused us . . .' He mopped his

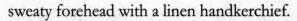

sweaty forehead with a linen handkerchief.

Mrs Abbott was smiling politely, but Olivia's dad was pondering a silk screen of birds flying over a river.

The moment they joined the group, Mrs Abbott interrupted. 'Oh, Olivia, sweetheart. Have you met George and Katrina?'

Katrina looked bored out of her mind.

'Lovely to meet you,' Olivia said to the bald man and his wife.

'Olivia is my daughter,' Mrs Abbott said, pulling Olivia in for a side-hug. 'She was in the movie!'

'Uh, well done,' said George, uncomfortably. Olivia wondered if he'd even watched it. 'I should go and find Edgar.'

Once the couple had disappeared into the crowd, Mr Abbott said, 'I'm so glad you came over then. Like a babbling brook, that man.'

'Behave,' Mrs Abbott said, swatting his arm. 'Now, Jackson, is this the first time you've been carved into a block of ice?'

Olivia noticed that the ice-Jackson's nose was dripping, but it did really look like him.

'It is,' Jackson replied, 'but apparently in two weeks, I'm going to be even bigger than that.'

'Mount Rushmore?' Mr Abbott asked, joking.

'Actually, a balloon float just outside the *Bright Stars* awards show,' Jackson replied. 'I'm hosting.'

'Hosting!' Olivia couldn't believe it. The *Bright Stars*? She had watched the whole two-hour show for the past three years running. It featured all the most glamorous and popular young celebrities – musicians, sports people and actors, as voted for by the public. She had even voted for Jackson once or twice. Or maybe more than that.

'Mr and Mrs Abbott,' Jackson said, taking a formal tone. 'I would like to ask your permission to take Olivia as my date to the awards. You or Mr Vega could chaperone?'

Olivia wanted to do a back flip right then, but her dress was too long. She desperately hoped her parents would say yes.

Mrs Abbott clapped her hands. 'Oh, I'm sure we could work something out. How wonderful!'

'And . . .' Jackson said. 'I believe there's a chance my beautiful girlfriend may be in the running for an award.'

'Eee!' Olivia couldn't hold back the squeal that emerged. She felt part-excited, part-nauseous. To be on stage receiving an award? It was more than a girl from Franklin Grove could hope for – and it was the scariest thing Olivia had ever imagined.

'Joy and trepidation spread like rays of the sun,' quipped Mr Abbott.

'But . . . don't you have to be famous to do that?' Olivia wondered.

Jackson smiled. 'Up-and-coming famous is good enough for the shortlisting committee.'

Mrs Abbott gave Olivia a nudge. 'That would be you!'

'I've been in one movie!'

'Well, I can't promise,' said Jackson, 'it's only a rumour I've heard.'

Before Olivia could reply, a blur of yellow dress and red hair interrupted.

'News!' said Amy Teller, flapping her gold-bangled arms. 'I've got news!'

'Hello, Amy,' said Mrs Abbott.

'Mrs Abbott. Steve. Lovely to see you,' said Amy, air-kissing them quickly. She turned back to Jackson and Olivia. 'This is big. It's going to be HUGE!'

Olivia had never seen Amy so excited. Normally, she was shouting down the phone or frowning at some poor underling who'd got something wrong.

'I've just been roped into negotiations by Jacob Harker about . . .' Amy paused for suspense. 'You!' she said, looking straight at Olivia.

'Me?' Olivia was baffled. What would the head of the studio want with her? 'Did I say "totally" too much in the movie? Or was I touching my hair?' Had she flopped?

'No, silly!' Amy said. 'He just loves you and wants you for the filming of *Eternal Sunset* – the biggest blockbuster in pre-production. I said, "Well, my client is going to need some special billing," and he said –'

'Your client?' Olivia interrupted.

'You practically *are* my client at this point, right?' Amy waved her hand. 'We'll take care of the paperwork later.' She was talking so fast Olivia could barely keep up. Harker thought she was star material!

'Apparently, there's some other newcomer

actress playing your twin sister but – get this! – the fool is negotiating her own contract.' Amy cackled with laughter. 'Can you imagine how naive someone would have to be to try that in Hollywood?'

Olivia felt like she'd just won prom queen. She wondered for a moment who the other actress could be.

'Do you know who it is?' Jackson asked.

'Some wannabe,' she replied. 'Harker didn't say who, but does it matter? I've just landed Olivia a huge role!'

Jackson cleared his throat. 'I think Olivia has landed herself a huge role.'

For an instant, Amy looked guilty. 'Oh ... I ... uh ...'

'But,' Olivia put in quickly, 'I am glad for your help. After all, if Jackson chose you as his agent, then you must be the best.'

Amy beamed. 'Aw, thanks. Now, we are going to make you huge!'

Jackson and the Abbotts looked delighted. Olivia gazed at the room full of producers and agents.

How has it happened that I'm part of this world? she marvelled.

Amy was babbling on about contracts and riders.

Whatever had happened to set this all in motion, Olivia was grateful. She'd always wanted to act professionally. This could be her big chance!

Chapter Five

Six days later, the sun was shining. Birds were chirping, chickens were clucking at her feet and Ivy didn't mind in the slightest. Usually, vampires didn't like this amount of sunlight or being near animals but, for today, Ivy was prepared to make an exception.

She and Olivia were with their dad at Aunt Rebecca's ranch in Beldrake for a barbecue. Ever since the two of them had come to visit here a few weeks ago, it had become a home-from-home. The stables, the farmhouse, the big willow tree, the lake with the ducks: it was so picturesque.

Their mother had stayed here every summer as a girl, and just being here made Ivy feel closer to her.

It was a relief to finally dress down again after the premiere and the party last week. The only people she'd see today were family and friends. Thank darkness!

She was especially happy that she'd have space from Harker. *All he wants to do is offer me movie roles!* Ivy was definitely feeling the guilt of not telling her sister what had been going on. There had barely been a free minute all week.

Ivy was determined to find the right time today to tell all.

'I can't believe you eat that stuff!' Aunt Rebecca said. She was standing at the barbecue holding a spatula, next to Mr Vega, who had his own spatula for the meat. Rebecca was wearing faded jeans, heavy black riding boots and a yellow checked apron over her flannel shirt.

Mr Vega was lightly grilling the steaks for the meat-eaters while Rebecca was roasting halloumi for the vegetarians, herself and Olivia.

'My mouth is watering with anticipation,' Mr Vega replied with a smile.

'Mine, too!' Ivy called over from the table.

Ivy was relieved that Aunt Rebecca and her dad had put the past behind them. A few weeks ago, Ivy and Olivia didn't even know that they had an aunt, let alone that their mother had a twin sister. When Mr Vega made a special trip to track down their aunt and heal old wounds, the reunion hadn't been exactly warm.

But now they were a big happy family: vampires, humans, horses, chickens and Gibson and Gonzo, the two black Labradors. Ivy had even managed to feel almost – almost! – comfortable around all the animals. Especially after helping track down a runaway horse, she'd started to believe that her vampire blood didn't have to get in the way of helping on the farm.

Ivy took a break from chopping up the new carrots for the salad to peer at the barbecue. There were at least ten steaks and half a dozen veggie burgers. 'I do like steak, but even I can't eat more than one. There's way too much meat on that barbecue.'

'Ah, but you don't know what I know,' replied her dad.

'Or what I know,' said Rebecca. They shared a smile.

'Uh oh,' Olivia said, from the other side of the table. 'There's a look in their eyes – and I've been slicing way too many cucumbers for the four of us.'

'So the big question is,' Ivy said, 'who else is coming?'

A horn tooted from the dusty driveway. As the

vehicle got closer, Ivy could make out at least five people in the big SUV.

When it came to a stop, the door flew open and out jumped Bethany, Brendan's little sister, followed by Brendan and his parents, Jackson and Lillian.

'Killer!' said Ivy, delighted.

'We thought we'd make an occasion of it,' said Aunt Rebecca, waving everyone over. 'After all, it's not every day that my nieces are in a movie. I wanted to celebrate!'

Olivia leaped up from the table, knocking over a neat stack of sliced cucumber. 'Oh, thank you!' She hurried over to greet the newcomers.

Jackson grabbed Olivia in a hug and Brendan came over to kiss Ivy on the cheek.

'Hello, gorgeous,' he said with a triumphant smile. He was clearly proud of himself for keeping Rebecca's impromptu party a surprise.

'Hi,' Ivy replied.

'Come on, guys,' said Bethany. 'Enough of the mushy stuff – I want to meet the horses!' Bethany was Ivy's favourite seven-year-old. She was wearing blue jeans with a pink flower appliqué, and brown knee-high boots, perfect for horse riding.

Aunt Rebecca smiled. 'My kind of girl,' she said to Bethany. 'But let's wait until we're done eating so I can give you a proper introduction. How about you go and say hello to my ducks, instead?'

'We've a lot of food to get through,' Mr Vega said.

Bethany considered for a moment. 'OK, but only if I get to pick which steak is mine.'

Mr and Mrs Daniels laughed and shook hands with Aunt Rebecca.

'Thanks for inviting us with Brendan,' said Mrs

Daniels. 'Bethany thinks she's won the lottery!'

Lillian hung back a little. She was wearing black jeans with black ankle boots and a black-and-grey checked sweater – almost like a cool vamp-farmer.

Mr Vega hurried over and said, 'Excuse the grease, Lillian. I'm so glad you could come.' He leaned in for a cheek-kiss, at the same time as Lillian went for one on the opposite cheek, so there was a little awkwardness because they almost kissed.

Mr Vega blushed and Lillian chuckled. They tried again, and got it right.

'You made it!' Rebecca said to Lillian. 'I just had to meet the woman who was so inspired by Charles that she hired his design services.'

'Thanks for inviting me.' Lillian pulled a packet, wrapped in brown paper, out of her big black bag and handed it to Rebecca. 'Charles said that you used to live in LA, so I thought these might remind you of home.'

Ivy was impressed that Lillian had brought a present. Rebecca opened it and Ivy peered over to see what it was. It was a little envelope with seeds labelled Ceanothus Joyce Coulter.

'I know these!' exclaimed Rebecca. 'It's that gorgeous blue mountain lilac. Native to California, right?'

Lillian nodded.

Rebecca smiled at Lillian. 'We are going to be good friends, you and I. Now, where do you live in LA?'

The adults were all happy chatting and Bethany was occupying herself tearing up a loaf of bread and tossing it to the ducks, with Jackson and Brendan helping by stuffing chunks of bread in their own mouths. Ivy realised it was the perfect moment to talk to Olivia.

Ivy scooted around the table with her carrots and started chopping next to her sister. 'So . . .' she began, feeling a little nervous.

'So?' Olivia replied, pausing mid-slice.

'I've wanted to talk to you about something, but the past week has been so manic.' Ivy knew she should just come out with it, but she didn't know if it would upset her sister.

'OK,' Olivia said, returning to her chopping.

'You know *Eternal Sunset*?' Ivy said.

Olivia beamed. 'I am so, so excited. I have always loved those books and can't believe I might have a chance to play Carmina!'

Ivy knew this meant the world to Olivia. 'And then you know that there has to be a Belinda as well.'

'Of course! Amy is trying to find out who it is.' Olivia sliced away. 'Although it will be weird to have a sister that isn't you.'

Ivy cleared her throat.

'Wait a minute,' Olivia said. 'What's going on?'

Ivy smiled sheepishly. 'It's me.'

'You!' The knife clattered on to the plastic chopping board.

'Harker totally loves you and thinks it's a genius plan to surprise the whole world with me as your twin when he announces the movie,' Ivy rushed out.

Olivia squealed and gave Ivy a huge hug. 'We get to be twins on screen! Oh, it will be so much better having you *and* Jackson by my side. This is amazing.'

'But, Olivia,' Ivy protested. 'I can't act. I'm as wooden as a stake.'

'Um . . .' Olivia winced. Ivy didn't even mind that she wasn't disagreeing; she knew it was true.

'I'm happy behind the camera,' Ivy said, 'but

I'll be the worst Belinda possible if Harker goes through with this.'

'So, why haven't you told Harker this?' Olivia asked, confusion filling her big green eyes.

'I tried, but he wouldn't listen.' Ivy sighed. 'The truth is, if I'm not in the movie, then you won't be either. Harker insists it's the two of us or nothing.'

Olivia sucked in her breath. 'So you're doing this just for me.'

'And there's another catch,' Ivy went on. 'If the bunny press catch wind that you and I are twins and ruin Harker's big announcement, he says he'll call the whole thing off.'

Olivia stared at Ivy, her eyes brimming. 'We don't have to go through with this, you know. I don't want to force you into doing something you'd hate.'

'I want you to have your shot,' Ivy said,

determined, 'but I also don't want to humiliate myself or you if Harker sees me acting.'

All the sparkle had gone from her sister's eyes.

'We just need a plan.' Ivy looked down at her decapitated carrots. 'A way to show Harker that you are perfect for the movie, but I'm not. Then he might see sense and let me off the hook.'

Jackson came over, and planted a kiss on the top of Olivia's head. 'What are you two talking about?'

But before they could reply, Brendan shouted angrily. 'Hey!'

He was looking over towards the fence beyond the main drive.

'What was that?' Ivy muttered.

'Get out of here!' Jackson shouted.

Mr Daniels and Ivy's dad raced to the edge of the property, with Aunt Rebecca chasing after them. A man on a motorcycle with a black helmet, red streaked jacket and long-lens camera revved his engine loudly, making the ducks squawk and scatter. Then he peeled away in a cloud of dust.

'Hey! Stop!' shouted Rebecca, but of course he didn't.

'Oh no,' whispered Ivy. Their peaceful family barbecue had been invaded. 'Do you think he got a picture of us together?' If he did, the whole movie thing could be ruined.

'Or of me and Jackson,' Olivia said, biting her lip.

'This feels awful,' Ivy said. 'Like I've been robbed or something.'

As the adults came back, Jackson said, 'Photographers. They're worse than bloodsucking vampires.'

'He must have followed our car here,' Brendan guessed.

Bethany had her hands on her hips. 'Meanie! He scared off the ducks.'

Brendan gave Bethany a hug. 'Don't worry. We'll tempt them back with more bread.'

'I'm really sorry,' Jackson said.

'If this keeps up, we're going to have to do something about it,' Mr Vega replied, frowning.

'There are things you can do,' Lillian replied. 'They are only allowed to photograph public figures, and Jackson's the only one here who falls into that category. If they print photos of private citizens, you can take legal action.'

Ivy sighed. Hollywood was taking over her life.

🦇　　　🦇　　　🦇

The next day, Olivia was perched on a beige sofa with bright lights shining down on her. Franklin Grove Middle School had allowed a TV company to set up a makeshift studio in a classroom over the weekend, in order to interview their student.

'As a one-off favour,' the head teacher had said.

The TV crew had totally transformed the room.

The desks had been moved to the back and a fake wall with wallpaper had been pushed in front of the white board. It looked just like a real living room.

'I don't think I have to remind you how important this interview could be,' said Amy Teller, her mobile phone clutched in her hand like a lifeline. She was sitting in the opposite seat, where the host would be in less than ten minutes. 'You cannot let on about Ivy, in any way.'

Olivia nodded. 'I know.'

Harker had decided that Olivia would become the star of the initial marketing for *Eternal Sunset*. She'd been set up for an exclusive interview that would go out to the nation that evening. But Olivia had to keep Ivy's identity a secret so that they could reveal the whole twin-thing for another big headline grabber. *Lucky for Ivy, really*, Olivia thought. Her sister hated being in the limelight and an interview like this might just break her out in boils.

Lucky for me, Olivia thought, *I love this kind of thing!*

'And not a word about Jackson,' Amy reminded her.

'I know,' Olivia said through gritted teeth. She wished they weren't still keeping their relationship a secret, but at the same time, she didn't want anyone to think she only got her big role because of her connection to him.

'Three minutes!' called out a young woman wearing a headset. There were two people running around with clipboards, at least six cameras and lots of lighting equipment. One guy was testing the TV that was hanging right behind Olivia's head.

Amy stood up. 'I'll be right over there.' She pointed to desk chairs just beyond the fake wooden flooring. 'If you get into a panic, just work some kind of code word into the conversation.'

'Code word?' Olivia echoed.

'How about "famous"?' Amy suggested. 'Yes, do that. Just say "famous" and I'll step in.' Then she winked. 'That's what agents do; we protect our clients!'

'Two minutes!' called Headset Lady. Even though there were only a handful of people making the show, soon thousands would be watching on TV.

Olivia managed a smile as even more lights turned on her.

'You look great!' Amy whispered and then clicked away on her high black heels.

Olivia had chosen a three-quarter sleeve, light pink dress with a short white sweater over it. The sweater was a little more girly than Olivia would normally go for, but she was trying to get into Carmina's character.

The classroom door opened. 'You must be Olivia!' said a darkly handsome man with perfect white teeth. It was Chuck Talbot, the famous TV host from *Inside Hollywood*. He sat down across from her and put a note card on the little glass table between them.

The butterflies were doing round-offs in her stomach. *This is it!* Olivia thought.

'What a story you've got, young lady,' Chuck said. 'Being plucked from the street to star in one of the biggest movies ever! You are going to be an inspiration to millions of girls.' Chuck smiled.

Olivia beamed.

'We're rolling in ten seconds.' A silence fell over the classroom. 'Three . . . two . . . one . . .'

'Hi, I'm Chuck Talbot and today I have with

me Olivia Abbott, a Hollywood rags-to-riches story that most people only dream about.'

Not exactly rags to riches, Olivia thought, but she kept the smile on her face.

'Tell me about how you came to be chosen for the most eligible role around, as Carmina of *Eternal Sunset*?' Chuck looked at her expectantly.

'Well,' Olivia began, 'my first film was *The Groves –*'

'With the ever dreamy Jackson Caulfield,' interrupted Chuck.

Olivia caught sight of Amy looking tense in the corner. She decided to steer the conversation away from her boyfriend. 'That's right. And when the Carmina role came up, they thought I might be a good fit.'

'The perfect fit, more like!' said Chuck enthusiastically. 'Tell me about this!'

He turned to the TV screen and Olivia saw a

huge shot of herself posing at the premiere in Spencer's altered dress.

'All we know is that a friend designed it for you.' Chuck made air quotes when he said 'friend'.

Olivia grinned. Now was as good a time as any to give Spencer the exposure he deserved. 'Everyone knows the amazing Spencer Johnson, make-up artist extraordinaire.'

Chuck nodded eagerly.

'Well, all I can say is that his talents are boundless!' Olivia said.

Chuck turned to the camera. 'You heard it here first, folks! An exclusive reveal of the brains behind Olivia's trend-setting red-carpet look!'

Olivia smiled to herself, wondering if that meant everyone would want to be spilling coffee on their evening wear.

She noticed Amy giving her a thumbs-up from behind the cameras.

'Now, Olivia.' Chuck leaned closer. 'The question everyone wants to know is . . . who is the mystery actress who will be playing Belinda opposite you? I hear the paparazzi have been close on your heels, trying to photograph you with anyone who might be a fellow actress.'

Olivia took a deep breath. 'My lips are sealed.'

'But you know who it is?' Chuck insisted.

Olivia wondered if now was the time to push the panic button. 'I'm afraid that's one exclusive that I can't give you just yet.'

'Yet?' Chuck was practically drooling.

Olivia didn't want to make any promises that she couldn't keep. 'It's all hush hush right now, but I'll see what I can do about telling you first.'

'A true star.' Chuck looked like he'd just been given an award. 'What's been the hardest thing about rocketing to fame?'

Olivia frowned. She didn't want to seem

ungrateful. She was enjoying almost everything, but there was one thing. 'The photographers are very insistent.'

Chuck grinned. 'That's a mild way of putting it.'

Olivia shrugged. 'I know everyone has a job to do, but they seem to step over the line.'

Chuck turned to the camera. 'You paparazzi, you hear that? You leave my lovely friend Olivia alone!'

Olivia laughed. 'That's right. I'll tell them Chuck said so.'

'Yes, I did!' he declared. 'It was lovely to meet you, Olivia, and I'll see you back on that sofa soon to spill all the beans about the mystery actress.'

'CUT!' shouted Headset Lady.

'That was great,' Chuck said. 'You're a natural.'

Olivia was relieved and proud of herself at the same time. She hadn't slipped up on anything and Chuck actually seemed to like her. This was how she was hoping this movie stuff would turn out to be.

Amy hurried over, clapping. 'You did great, sweetie!'

'Chuck,' said Headset Lady, 'it's time for the skateboarding kitten intro.'

Chuck waved goodbye, and Olivia walked out of the studio feeling exhilarated.

'Good stuff,' said Headset Lady, as she passed.

Olivia had just survived her first big interview!

🦇　　　🦇　　　🦇

'Can we suspend the no-biting-humans rule just for this week?' Sophia whispered, making sure no one else in the busy school cafeteria but Ivy and Brendan could hear. 'They are driving me crazy!'

Ivy had thought no one could be as angry as she was about the photographers that were camped out all over town. Since yesterday's interview, there were even more of them. Some of them were peering in the cafeteria windows right at this moment. If Sophia was talking about reverting to the old vampire ways, she must be outraged.

The one paparazzo on the motorcycle at Aunt Rebecca's had multiplied into a swarm that never let up. They were desperate for a photo of the mystery actress, but there was every danger they'd also catch Jackson and Olivia together.

'*I'm* the Franklin Grove correspondent!' Sophia complained. 'All of these brutes are stealing my exclusivity!'

'On the bright side, you are the only one that could get close enough to get a shot of that ketchup on Ivy's cheek,' Brendan said, pointing to the left side of her mouth.

'Wha—!' Ivy grabbed a napkin and wiped her face.

They all chuckled.

'It would be just my luck that a photo with ketchup smeared all over my face would be the one that exposes me to the whole world.' Ivy was feeling more and more panicky at the pressure that was building in the lead-up to whatever announcement Harker had planned.

'You'll figure something out,' Brendan said. 'Are you going to eat that?' He pointed to Ivy's half-eaten burger and fries.

Ivy shook her head and pushed it over to him. The photographers were bound to catch her and Olivia together, figure out that they are twins and run a picture in a magazine – then it would be all over.

Just then, a guy wearing a faded grey hoodie, sunglasses and cowboy boots plunked his tray down on the table. Ivy might have mistaken him for some slacker, but she'd seen those cowboy boots often enough.

'Hey guys,' said Jackson from under the hood.

'Hey,' said Brendan with his mouth full.

Sophia scooted over so Jackson could sit down. Ivy wondered what was keeping Olivia.

'I've been stalking the stalkers and it seems someone has tipped them off about *Eternal Sunset*'s mystery second actress living in Franklin Grove.' Jackson pushed his sunglasses down his nose and looked at Ivy with his blue eyes. 'They are haunting every school, café and cinema, hoping to track down an exclusive.'

Ivy groaned and Sophia growled.

'There's a mole,' Ivy said.

'With half of Hollywood hanging around for the premiere, it could be anybody,' Jackson said.

'The instant they see Olivia and me together, they'll know,' Ivy said. 'If they don't already.'

Two tables away, Ivy caught sight of Charlotte Brown and her cronies.

'Jessica says that you should definitely *not* wear a mini skirt with ankle socks,' Charlotte practically shouted, so that the whole cafeteria could hear. 'You have to wear knee-highs.' She'd been going around all week telling everyone how she and Jessica were now BFFs.

Ugh, Ivy thought.

'No prize for guessing how they got tipped off,' Ivy said, putting her face in her hands. 'And it's totally my fault.' Ivy remembered the victorious feeling of accepting Harker's offer in front of Jessica and all those suits, but her enemy must have put two and two together and realised exactly which film Ivy was due to star in. That moment of triumph could cost Olivia big time.

'We've got to do something,' Ivy declared.

'Yes, please!' replied Sophia.

'I'll help,' Jackson put in.

'Could we trap them in the school and force them to take our math quiz?' Brendan joked, with his mouth full of burger.

'I like that idea,' Jackson said. 'I haven't studied.'

'Focus, please!' interrupted Ivy. 'First, we need to make sure that Olivia and I aren't seen together and, second, we need to throw the paps off the scent.'

But before Ivy could come up with a plan, she spotted her sister wandering into the cafeteria.

Disaster alert! Ivy realised. The photographers still had their noses pressed up against the window.

Olivia spotted them at their table. If Ivy didn't do something about it, Olivia would blow their cover.

She leaped up from her seat. 'STOP!' she shouted at the top of her lungs.

Olivia stopped dead in the doorway, confused, and a hundred student heads swivelled to stare at Ivy.

Ivy tried to ignore them, but she noticed Charlotte watching her carefully. She couldn't let Charlotte figure out what she was up to, so she turned to Brendan.

'Stop stealing my ketchup!' she shouted. 'You know how much it means to me.'

Sophia sniggered and Brendan dropped the three fries that were halfway to his mouth. Charlotte rolled her eyes and went back to tittering with her minions.

Ivy looked over at Olivia, who seemed to realise that something was going on. She took a step forwards and Ivy shook her head fiercely.

Her sister got the point and stepped back while Ivy grabbed her history book and shielded her face from the window where the photographers were.

'She can't come in here,' Ivy said. 'Not looking like that.'

'Like what?' Sophia asked.

'Like me, of course!' Ivy said.

Jackson scowled, and looked a little intimidating with his hoodie and sunglasses. 'I'm going to talk to the principal before next period, see if we can get them to stay away from the school.'

'That would be a relief,' Ivy said. 'But they'll just be waiting outside for when we leave.'

Ivy saw Olivia waving from the doorway. She pointed to the food line and then to her belly and mouthed, 'I'm hungry!'

'Poor Olivia,' said Jackson. 'We can't let her starve.'

He stood up and went over to the counter, grabbing a salad, a bagel sandwich and a brownie on a tray for Olivia and then sat with her right there in the doorway, having lunch, as bemused fellow students walked around them to get into the cafeteria. The photographers' lenses couldn't see around the pillars at the entrance. They were safe for now.

'I've got an idea. Code black, right after school,' Ivy said, invoking her and Sophia's age-old code for meeting in the science hall bathroom.

Sophia nodded but Brendan said, 'Uh . . . what does that mean?'

Ivy smiled. 'Have you ever wanted to visit the girl's bathroom?'

Chapter Six

Twenty minutes after school, Olivia was waiting in the girls' bathroom for Sergeant Ivy to give her orders. Ivy had assembled Sophia, Camilla, Brendan and Jackson as well and had stuck a sign on the bathroom door that said OUT OF ORDER.

'This is weirder than weird,' said Brendan, looking around at the green-painted cubicles.

'Agreed,' said Jackson. 'What if someone comes in?'

Olivia giggled. 'Soon it won't matter.'

'I can't believe I've agreed to this,' Brendan

said, shaking his head.

'Atten-tion!' Ivy said. 'Let's get a move on. Camilla?'

Camilla stepped forwards and emptied a big box on to the bathroom counter, spilling out wigs, sunglasses, expensive-looking bags, blouses and fake jewellery.

Brendan's eyes almost popped out of his head.

'I've still got the key to the costume room,' Camilla explained with a shrug.

'Begin!' Ivy ordered.

While everyone started picking through the offerings, Olivia handed Ivy the clothes out of her bag.

Ivy quickly sprayed herself down with some fake tan, slipped on the denim skirt, lavender sweater and white sandals – the exact same outfit as Olivia had on. 'There,' she said to her sister. 'Olivia the second, at your service.'

'Not quite,' Olivia replied. 'Olivia would never forget to accessorise!' She took a chunky white bead necklace from the counter and put it around Ivy's neck. 'Better.'

Olivia caught sight of herself and her twin next to each other in the mirror. Sometimes they looked like night and day with their different skin tones and dress sense. But at times like this, when they were switching, it showed how much, underneath it all, they were just the same – sisters and best friends.

'No matter what,' Olivia said to Ivy amid the chaos of the bathroom, 'we'll figure this thing out.'

'But *we* won't!' Brendan called from the other end of the counter with Jackson. He was holding a long black wig in his right hand and a short blond one in his left. He had four different necklaces around his neck and was wearing a loose pink shirt with a long green skirt. 'Help!'

Olivia cracked up and Ivy joined in, holding her hands to her stomach.

'No one is going to believe you're a movie star!' Ivy said.

'Hey,' said Brendan defensively, 'this was your idea.'

Ivy kissed him on the nose. 'I know, and it's going to work too.'

'But not with you looking like that!' Olivia declared. She handed Brendan an oversized blue sweater. 'Pink is definitely not your colour. Lose the shirt.'

Brendan eagerly complied, ripping off the shirt and flexing his muscles.

'And since you don't exactly fit the body-shape of an up-and-coming female star . . .' Olivia went on, 'we'll have to aim for as much distraction as possible.' She handed over a long blond wig and white sunglasses.

Ivy's plan for Operation Escape was to have lots of possible mystery actresses to throw the creepy photographers off the real trail.

Olivia and a glammed-up Camilla were going to form one pair to lead off as many paps as they could, while Ivy-as-Olivia and Brendan-as-mysterious-movie-star led the rest in the opposite direction. Jackson would play himself with a Hollywood-ised Sophia as a third possibility. Ivy's plan was that the photographers would become so confused and fed up that they'd give up and go back to California.

'What are you going to do about the shoes?' Camilla asked, pointing at Brendan's huge steel-toed boots.

'Well, I can't wear little sandals,' Brendan declared. 'I haven't had my pedicure.' He and Jackson cracked up and Ivy rolled her eyes.

'Your hairy toes would give you away,' she shot back.

'How about these?' Camilla said. They were pink sneakers that looked just about big enough.

'They don't exactly go with my outfit,' Brendan teased. 'But they'll be good for when we have to run.'

'They will have to do,' Ivy replied. As Brendan hopped around, putting on the sneakers, she barked out her orders. 'We need to divide, conquer, and confuse the paparazzi until they give up.'

When Brendan finally stopped hopping, Ivy called out, 'Troops, line up!'

Olivia obeyed, along with everyone else. Her five friends stood to attention in front of the bathroom mirror.

Sophia, standing next to Jackson, was wearing all black, with huge black sunglasses, red lipstick

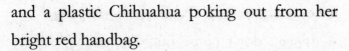

and a plastic Chihuahua poking out from her bright red handbag.

'Check,' Ivy said.

Beside Olivia, Camilla was wearing a broad-brimmed straw hat, a white floaty dress with Grecian sandals and had a copy of the script for *Romezog and Julietron*, a sci-fi version of Shakespeare's, *Romeo and Juliet*, which she'd recently directed.

'Check,' Ivy said again.

Ivy marched to the end of the line and slipped her arm through Brendan's. He looked utterly ridiculous, but in that eccentric Hollywood way. Olivia smiled – even dressed up all strange, they were a perfect couple.

'Ready?' Ivy asked everyone.

But before everyone could reply, there was a clank from inside one of the bathroom cubicles.

Olivia whipped her head around and a hush

fell over her friends. *There's someone else in here!*

'If you don't come out, I'm going to start opening doors,' Ivy called out.

Olivia heard an exasperated sigh and the click of a lock.

Out stepped Charlotte Brown, looking sheepish. 'Whatever,' she said, when she saw everyone glaring at her. 'You people are crazy.' She was trying to hide something behind her back, but Ivy could see in the mirror. It was a disposable camera. Olivia realised that she must have been trying to do the same thing as the paparazzi!

'You little sneak!' Ivy said, about to lunge forwards, but Brendan put a hand on her arm.

Jackson stepped over, calmly, and held out an open palm. 'I'll have that, please.'

Olivia couldn't believe that Charlotte had been spying on them!

'What?' Charlotte said, faking innocence.

Jackson didn't say another word, just looked at her. Charlotte tossed her hair and shoved the camera into his hand. 'I couldn't get anything good anyway.'

'I can't believe you'd do this to a fellow cheerleader,' Olivia said quietly. The truth was that Charlotte had tried to cross her tons of times before, but never quite so publicly.

'It could have been worse,' Charlotte countered. 'I could have told the newspapers days ago that Ivy's the mystery actress they're all so interested in.'

'So why didn't you?' Jackson asked, folding his arms.

Charlotte shrugged, clearly trying to look as though she couldn't care less. 'I tried. But they wouldn't pay the fee I was demanding.'

Jackson spluttered. 'You're priceless,' he said. 'Let me give you a tip about negotiation with newspapers. *They* set the price, not you.'

Olivia felt her face draining of blood. How could one girl be this nasty? Suddenly, she heard a whispering from the next stall. *It doesn't take a genius to figure out who's in there*, she thought. 'Hi, Katie, hi, Allison. Come out, please.'

The middle cubicle door opened and out struggled Katie and Allison, who had crowded in together. They both had disposable cameras in their hands.

'I'll have those,' Brendan said, taking the two other cameras. 'There will be no photographic evidence of my transformation – let alone photos of Ivy and Olivia together.'

'You mean you don't want people to see your freak show,' Charlotte said, crossing her arms.

Olivia realised there was something odd about Charlotte's skirt.

Charlotte's black skirt looked like it had been

shredded in a semi-circle – just like Olivia's ruined skirt from the premiere.

'What happened to your outfit?' Ivy demanded.

'Don't you know anything about fashion?' Charlotte huffed. 'Get out of the graveyard and into the real world.'

'Uh, Charlotte,' Ivy began, but Charlotte was on a roll.

'You don't deserve a role in any movie,' she sneered. 'And no amount of fake tan will stop you looking totally washed out on screen.'

'Hey,' Olivia started but Charlotte pushed past Jackson and right out through the bathroom door, Katie and Allison scurrying after her.

When the door closed, Ivy sighed. 'She's right, you know. I only got this role because of my big mouth. I don't want the gig and I don't deserve it.'

Olivia felt awful. Everything was so complicated!

'Look,' said Brendan. 'Let's deal with one problem at a time. We'll get rid of the photographers and then worry about the movies.'

Ivy nodded and Olivia decided she had to focus on Operation Escape.

'Now,' he went on, 'are you going to help me with this lipstick?'

Ivy peered out from behind the school doors. Other students shot her curious glances as they left school for the day.

Phase one of Operation Escape was under way. Jackson, still in his hoodie, and Sophia, looking gorgeous, were hurrying down the steps, deep in conversation.

'This itches,' Brendan complained from his place behind Ivy. She looked round; he was scratching under his wig.

'You're stepping on my foot!' hissed Camilla.

'Sshh!' Ivy said.

Ivy turned back to watch the scene outside the school building. As Jackson and Sophia arrived at the bottom of the steps, Ivy could see the paparazzi gathered at the end of the path.

One of them had the same jacket with the red streak as the guy who had been stalking them at Aunt Rebecca's ranch.

The photographers started elbowing each other and whispering, as they caught a peek of Jackson's famous face from beneath his hood. Ivy could almost *see* the rumour travelling through the crowd! Then Jackson threw the hood back so they could really see who he was.

'Is that the actress?' one shouted and they all started snapping away, just as Ivy had hoped.

Jackson pretended to try and shield Sophia from the cameras, and she squealed and hid behind her bag.

Bingo! 'They're playing it perfectly,' Ivy murmured. The two of them dashed through the crowd of photographers, with several in pursuit as they headed towards the Meat and Greet.

There were soon only five paps left hanging around, including Mr Red Jacket.

'Cue two!' Ivy whispered and waved Olivia and Camilla into place.

Olivia gave Ivy a quick hug. 'Thanks for going to all this trouble.' She smiled at Brendan. 'You get a special gold star.'

'Thanks,' he replied. 'This is a once-in-a-lifetime occurrence, and any and all material rewards will be gratefully accepted.'

Olivia gave a little wave as she and Camilla headed down the steps.

'Good luck,' Ivy whispered.

'It's Olivia!' one of the photographers shouted.

Olivia paused at the bottom of the steps and waved – just as they'd agreed. Then she hooked her arm through Camilla's and cooed at the cameras. 'This is my friend Venetia,' she declared.

'Is she off that TV show, *Blue Moon Rising*?' Mr Red Jacket shouted.

Camilla didn't say anything, just pretended to hide behind her hands when they started taking photos. Then Olivia and Camilla dashed in the opposite direction to Jackson, towards the mall. The group of five paparazzi followed them, trying to get a good shot of Olivia with her famous-looking friend.

'Our turn,' Ivy said to Brendan.

She stepped away from the door and they hurried through the hallway to the back entrance. When they were passing a set of lockers, a sixth grader stopped and stared at Brendan.

'I'm testing out Halloween costumes,' Brendan explained. 'What do you think?'

The sixth grader just blinked.

'Pretty scary, huh?' Brendan grinned and Ivy grabbed his arm.

'You only have to fool them for a couple of minutes,' Ivy reminded him. They were going to head to the mall and prepare for the Great Switcheroo.

They rushed along and pushed through the glass doors at the back, then darted around the side of the building. All of the photographers were gone, as planned, so Ivy and Brendan headed for their rendezvous point at the mall.

The only thing that couldn't happen was two Olivias being seen together or the game would be up.

'It's hard to run in a skirt,' Brendan commented as they dashed along the road, getting more than a few intrigued glances from the people they passed on the sidewalk.

'We're almost there,' Ivy replied, as the east entrance to the mall came into sight.

They hurried past the stores to the food court. Despite the absurdity of having to do it, Ivy couldn't help enjoying the chaos just a little.

Up ahead, she spotted the real Olivia and Camilla sprinting towards the bathroom with all five photographers still after them. She couldn't see Jackson and Sophia yet, but she was sure they were on their way.

Ivy and Brendan crouched behind a palm tree at the front of the food court and waited.

The paps lurked near the bathroom, waiting for any sign of Olivia and her mysterious friend.

There was a commotion from near the stationery store. It was Jackson and Sophia, with five more paparazzi in tow!

Sophia shouted in a fake British accent, 'These people are invading my privacy!'

'They won't leave us alone!' called Jackson.

The photographers that had been chasing Olivia and Camilla whirled around to capture whatever was happening.

The shoppers all turned to stare.

'Help us!' Jackson cried to a burly man with a bag from the Sewing Store.

He took one look at the mega-famous movie star and turned on the paparazzi, crossing his arms like an angry genie and blocking their path. Two paps got in a tangle, trying to run around him and a third got attacked by an old lady in a purple dress wielding her handbag.

'It's working!' Ivy whispered to Brendan.

'Wish I was out there with that lady,' Brendan replied, grinning.

A gaggle of young girls shrieked when they saw Jackson and rushed over, trampling past the fourth pap. He had no chance of a photo now. There was only one left.

He seemed intent on staying in pursuit of Sophia and Jackson, who were almost at the bathroom. Then, a group of parents with toddlers walked past on their way to a coffee shop, sweeping him away.

'Get out of the way!' Ivy heard him cry. 'I almost had an exclusive there!'

The five photographers near the bathroom were laughing at their colleagues, and still snapping away.

'What's going on here?' demanded an overweight man in a bright orange uniform. 'We don't want your sort in here!' It was the manager of the Hummus Are Us deli in the food court.

'We have the right to be here!' shouted a pap wearing a green sweater.

As they argued, Sophia and Jackson just had time to duck into the bathroom.

'Showtime,' said Ivy.

I may not be an actress, Ivy thought, *but if I have to, I can put on a performance.*

She shouted across to where the confused photographers were untangling themselves from the crowd.

'Hey, paps!' she shouted. 'That should teach you!' Then she turned on her heel and ran.

Ivy was hoping that the photographers would be convinced that Olivia had escaped and chase her and Brendan across the food court to catch up.

'Hey!' shouted Green Sweater. 'There they go!'

One glance over her shoulder, and Ivy could see the photographers following.

She and Brendan ran back the way they had

come, dodging a family of five, a delivery of beads to the bead shop, and the chocolate kiosk. When Ivy looked back she saw that Olivia's five paps had been joined by Jackson's five and now, as they headed out the east entrance to the mall, all ten photographers were in pursuit.

Exhilarated, Ivy shared a grin with Brendan. They were just turning a corner, out of sight of the paps. 'Race ya!' she said to her boyfriend, then put on a burst of vampire speed. Her powerful muscles worked overtime, going at least twice as fast as a human's.

Brendan was surprised, but then boosted his own speed and soon they were practically flying down the street towards the final battleground.

Two blocks later, Ivy checked behind her to see the paps only just turning the corner. She made sure they saw her, and ducked into Patsy's Pastry Shop, a cosy little store filled with wonderful baking smells, cupcakes with four-inch-high icing and fresh croissants.

'Yummy,' said Ivy. But she wasn't here for a leisurely hot chocolate. 'Two ham-and-cheese croissants, please, Patsy,' she said, not even out of breath from the run.

Any moment now the photographers were going to catch up.

Patsy Lovett, a large woman with big blonde hair, raised one eyebrow at the sight of Brendan's now straggly black wig, but she served up the croissants and handed them over.

Just as Brendan and Ivy were settling down, the paparazzi caught sight of them in the shop window. Mr Red Jacket shouted, 'There!' and pointed, which made Patsy frown.

They gathered at the window, shoving each other aside to get the first shot of 'Olivia' and the mystery actress.

'Hey!' Patsy shouted.

She grabbed her rolling pin. Ivy already knew that Franklin Grove's baker didn't like anyone — anyone! — messing with her business.

Just as Ivy had hoped, Patsy stormed out of the shop and let loose on the stalkers. 'What do you think you're doing? You'll drive away my customers!'

'This is public property,' one pap shouted back.

'If you don't get away from my shop, I'll make room for those cameras in my oven.' Patsy looked like she meant it.

All but Mr Red Jacket scattered.

'I'm not doing anything illegal,' he protested.

Patsy advanced on him like she was stalking a mouse in her kitchen. 'But I might.'

Ivy saw the fear spread over his face and wanted to do one of Olivia's cheers. *P-A-T-S-Y !* *Patsy scares the mean paps guy!*

Patsy got right in his face, lifted one large finger and smudged flour on his nose. The pap yelped and scurried away.

Patsy came back in, dusting her hands off. 'Took care of that.'

'Thanks,' Ivy told her.

Brendan pulled off the wig. 'I don't think I'll be wearing this again any time soon.'

Moments later, Ivy saw Olivia, Camilla, Jackson and Sophia poking their heads around the real-estate office across the street. When they saw the coast was clear, they scurried inside the pastry shop. There wasn't a photographer in sight.

'It worked!' said Olivia, still a little out of breath.

'Thanks, everyone,' Ivy said, triumphant. 'Mission accomplished.'

Chapter Seven

After a round of Patsy's croissants, Olivia, Ivy, Camilla, Jackson, Brendan and Sophia headed to the Meat and Greet for celebratory milkshakes.

'That's definitely my exercise for the day,' Olivia said. 'I've earned a milkshake.'

Jackson smiled at her, making Olivia's heart pound as hard as when she'd been running from the paps. 'That was so much fun,' he said. 'I'd do the whole thing again!'

Ivy groaned. 'I hope that won't be necessary.'

Olivia bit her lip. They still hadn't figured out

how to fix this whole Harker mess. The longer Harker built up speculation about the other actress and waited to announce that they were twins, the more chances they had of being exposed.

'We may have escaped this time,' Olivia said, 'but they aren't going to stay away for long.'

Out of the corner of her eye, Olivia saw Charlotte sitting two booths away with someone, but Olivia couldn't see who. They were facing the other way.

Then Olivia heard a familiar voice coming from the booth. It was Jessica. 'You totally failed,' she was saying in a cold voice. 'You didn't get a single picture of the two of them and the paparazzi are furious for being given a false lead. They've given up and gone home! This is a disaster.'

Olivia nudged Ivy so that her sister would hear the conversation as well.

'If you   such an airhead, losing the camera, this wou   all worked!'

Olivia couldn't b   that sharp-tongued Charlotte was taking all o   is abuse without a single comeback.

'Without a photograph, I can't do anything. Not without risking my reputation – I need proof! You are a disgrace to all cheer captains everywhere,' Jessica declared, standing up. 'You are totally not cool enough to hang out with me.' Then she tossed her hair and marched off, leaving Charlotte looking miserable, shooting a disgusted look at Olivia as she went.

'Serves her right,' Ivy grumbled, but Olivia felt bad. Charlotte was the captain of her squad, after all. Olivia was just about to go over to Charlotte's booth to see if she was OK when someone burst through the doors of the Meat and Greet.

Olivia jumped, thinking that the paparazzi had

tracked them down. But it ... Amy Teller, for once without a phone o ... up of coffee in her hand, looking like she ... ast won a million dollars.

She rushed ov ... to their booth. 'We're going home!' she de...ared.

Every...e around the table stared at her.

'To Hollywood!' she cried. 'I've been looking everywhere for you.'

'For me?' asked Jackson.

'No, for my-new-favourite-client Olivia!' Amy beamed, gently pushing him out of the way.

Olivia gulped. Amy could be a little intense with her enthusiasm sometimes. 'Why me?' she asked.

'Because, you . . . and your sister . . .' Amy cast a quick glance over at Ivy and then did a double-take when she realised that it looked like there were two Olivias sitting at the table. 'Because the two of you will be flying out to Hollywood on Harker's private jet for the *Bright Stars* awards

ceremony
there; he's finally... He wants you both to be
roles in his new film!... break the news of your

'Wow,' said Camilla.

'So cool,' breathed Sophia.

Olivia couldn't stop the grin. 'A private jet?'

'Break the news?' Ivy echoed. Olivia could tell
she had mixed feelings about the announcement.
At least they wouldn't have to worry about being
exposed as twins, but it meant that she would be
committed to the movie.

'Your dad will be there, and Lillian is hitching a
ride as well,' Amy explained. 'And what about me,
you ask? Well,' she paused for dramatic effect. 'I
will be stepping off the plane and going *straight*
to a coffee shop. I can hardly wait!'

🦇　　　🦇　　　🦇

'This barely feels like an airplane,' Olivia
whispered to Ivy as she sat in a white leather

...und at the wood

designer armchair, ...een TV. 'It's more like

panelling and hu...at twenty thousand feet.'

a swanky livin...ve there's something that beats

'I can't ...

first-cla...avel to Europe!' Ivy replied, stuffing a

Californian sushi roll into her mouth. When they

had gone to meet their Transylvanian relatives,

their grandparents had paid for them to travel

first class.

Today, the private lounge at the airport had been huge and stocked with a fresh sandwich bar. Brendan had come to see them off and had a Philly cheese steak sub. Jackson had already flown out. He'd taken a day off school and left the day before for the award show's dress rehearsal.

Olivia glanced out of the window at puffy white clouds in a blue sky. *I am on my way to Hollywood!* she thought. Later that night, she would be attending a star-studded award ceremony with her movie-star boyfriend and she wouldn't have to keep the secret any more. It still felt a little unreal.

'More sushi?' asked the stewardess, poking her head through the curtain.

'Yes, please!' Ivy piped up.

Olivia stared at her. 'Well, it seems there are some things you could learn to live with.'

Ivy stuffed the last piece of sushi into her mouth and rolled her eyes at Olivia, making her laugh.

Olivia shook her head and gazed out of the tiny window at the ground far below.

'Hollywood, look out!' said Mr Vega. Olivia couldn't agree more. They were on their way!

In what seemed like no time at all, the private jet had landed and Olivia was following Mr Vega and Lillian out on to the tarmac, where a stretched black limo was waiting for them.

The bright sunshine felt warm on her skin after the cold air-conditioned plane, and the sky was bright blue.

'Miss Abbott,' said the chauffeur as he held the door for her. He was huge, and was probably more like a bodyguard than a chauffeur. 'I'm Frank.'

Once they were all settled in the luxurious back seat, Frank turned around and said, 'I hope you don't mind, folks, but Mr Harker has asked me to show you some of the sights.'

Olivia clapped her hands. 'A private tour!' she squealed.

'It seems we would like that very much,' said Mr Vega.

Frank set off, winding the mammoth car around the city streets. As they drove away from the airport, the scene changed from run-down houses to wide streets with plush green lawns and leafy trees.

'Most people think Hollywood is where all the glamour is,' Frank said. 'But actual Hollywood ain't pretty. The stars all live in Beverley Hills and that's where we are right now.'

The houses were huge and there were palm trees everywhere.

'Is this like your house?' Ivy asked Lillian.

'Ha!' Lillian replied. 'I have a teeny apartment on the other side of LA. These properties are for the mega-rich.'

Soon, they were driving past rows of stores.

'Oh, my pom poms!' Olivia squealed. 'That's Serendipity Fashion! And that's Kevin Greene! We're on Rodeo Drive!' She knew Ivy wouldn't be as excited, but she was glad to see her sister still smiling.

'Beverley Hills is six square miles of shopping, eating and luxurious living,' Frank went on. 'There are no hospitals and no cemeteries in the city limits, which means that, technically, no one is born or dies in Beverly Hills.'

'And that's not even counting the vampires,' Ivy whispered.

Olivia giggled. She wondered how many of the undead were wandering about in this town.

'Look at that dress!' Ivy declared, pointing out of the window at the Asante couture store. The dress on display was layers of rainbow colours with a huge u-shaped cut-out in the skirt – just like Spencer's creation.

'That's a rip-off of your skirt from the premiere,' said Lillian. 'And that girl there is wearing one, too.'

'Except no one had to spill latte on them, to make them look like that!' Olivia joked.

'Where Olivia goes,' Ivy teased, 'the rest of the world follows.'

Olivia took a deep breath. It was almost like an

unintended welcome. She could feel it; something big was going to happen this weekend.

🦇　　　🦇　　　🦇

'Why would anyone need three sinks in one bathroom?' Ivy asked.

'Why don't you just enjoy the luxury?' Olivia suggested.

Ivy sighed. The suite was so over-the-top that it made her feel uncomfortable: marble floors, floor-to-ceiling windows and an enormous bunch of fresh flowers in every room. All Ivy needed was a warm coffin somewhere to snuggle into.

Mr Vega and Lillian were in a meeting with Mr Harker about how his girls would be treated during filming. Ivy and Olivia were waiting for Frank to come and pick them up and take them on some mystery Hollywood adventure.

'I just want to say,' Olivia said, perching on the floral print chaise longue in the suite's sitting room. 'All this craziness isn't what it's about for me.'

'I know,' Ivy replied, taking a sip from her fluted glass of milkshake.

'Don't get me wrong, all this nice stuff is great.' Olivia grinned. 'But I want to do this because I think acting is the thing I'm really good at.'

'It is,' Ivy agreed. 'And that's why all these amazing things are happening for you. I'm just the black fly in your soup.'

Olivia sighed and Ivy felt that familiar pit of doom in her stomach.

'Harker's going to hate me the minute he gets me on set,' Ivy said. 'He doesn't realise that I'm no good. We've got to make him understand!'

'You know what?' Olivia said at last. 'It doesn't matter.'

'What do you mean?' Ivy asked.

'There will be other roles,' Olivia said. 'This crazy media baiting has nothing to do with making a good movie. Harker is just being dramatic.'

Ivy felt the pit filling in with a little bit of hope.

'I can't cope with all the secrets I've got to keep in this town. You. Jackson. So I'm just not going to worry about it any more,' Olivia declared. 'I'm going to enjoy this experience.'

There was a knock at the door. 'Ladies?' It was Frank. 'Ready to go?'

'Coming!' Olivia called. She grinned at Ivy. 'Let's be tourists and do some star-spotting!'

They grabbed their bags and hurried out into the hallway where Frank was waiting under a huge chandelier. He tipped his hat and they stepped into the mirrored elevator.

'Where are we going, Frank?' Ivy asked, checking her teeth in the mirror.

'I suppose I don't have to keep it secret any

longer,' he replied. 'To one of the biggest film studios in LA.'

'Which one?' Olivia wanted to know.

Frank grinned as the elevator door dinged open on to the underground parking lot. 'Rumour has it you might get to see the Killer Bees making their latest music video . . .'

Ivy gasped. The Killer Bees were one of her and Brendan's favourite bands!

'Or even the mega-famous Jackson Caulfield strolling around in-between takes,' Frank finished as he opened the door to their limo.

Ivy smiled. Of course, Frank wouldn't know that Olivia and Jackson were dating because it was still a big secret.

'The Killer Bees!' she whispered. Maybe this trip to Hollywood wouldn't be such a drag after all.

After a short drive, they pulled in through

some huge gates with a security guard peering in through their windscreen. There were warehouse buildings neatly lining a grid of streets, and people in golf carts zipping around. They drove past two men carrying an enormous Christmas tree and a woman dressed in an Elizabethan dress. It looked like chaos, but a lot of fun.

They pulled into a long parking space, designed just for limos.

Frank opened the door and helped them step out. 'Mr Harker will meet you in about half an hour, over on Lot 3.' He handed them a map of the huge complex. 'But until then, you can go anywhere you like.' He gave them two laminated passes with VIP written in big red letters.

Ivy kept scanning the crowd for any sign of James, Joe or John from the Killer Bees.

The map showed various studios and had little notes on their history.

'Ooh, that's where Wacky Walrus was made!' Ivy declared. 'I loved that show when I was little.'

Olivia laughed. 'Me too! Wa-cky Wal-rus likes to dance and sing . . .'

Ivy joined in for the second line, 'Wa-cky Walrus, he's the walrus king!'

Ivy squinted in the sun. 'I'm glad Lillian lent me her sun block. It's so hot!'

The sisters wandered across the sunny lot to the door marked VIP ONLY.

'Oooh.' Ivy played with the VIP pass around her neck, waving it in the air even though there was no one there to see it. 'VIP, that's me!' she said and Olivia giggled.

Her sister stuck her nose in the air. 'I'm very important, let me through!'

'Hey you!' shouted someone. 'You can't go in there!'

Olivia and Ivy swivelled around, their VIP

badges swinging from their cords.

It was a bald security man, and he did not look amused, but as soon as he saw their passes, he stopped. 'My apologies, ladies,' he said, backing off. 'Guests of Mr Harker are welcome anywhere.'

'Uh, thanks,' Ivy said. It was funny when they were pretending, but people bowing and scraping like that really made her uncomfortable.

Olivia pushed open the door to Studio 6 and Ivy followed her inside. The motion-sensor lights flickered on when they walked in to reveal a huge open space with wires snaking across the floor and random props everywhere.

'Look!' Olivia said, her voice echoing oddly in the emptiness.

She had found a display of Wacky Walrus merchandise and photographs behind the scenery. Olivia picked up one of the soft-toy versions of Wacky Walrus and made it dance through the air.

'Wa-cky Wal-rus,' she sang and Ivy joined in.

They started skipping around the studio, shouting the song louder and louder.

Olivia made Wacky Walrus sit on one of the tall, expensive-looking cameras and Ivy goofed around with a big soft-toy fish, making it swim up to Wacky and almost get eaten.

'You can't catch me, Mr Walrus King!' Ivy shouted, making the fish swim away.

Olivia shouted. 'Mm, tasty fish!' and chased Ivy over on to the stage area, which had a piano and big quilts hanging up on a laundry line.

'This totally reminds me of *The Parent Trap*!' Olivia said.

'Let's get together . . .' Ivy started, knowing she was off-key but not caring.

'Yeah, yeah, yeah!' finished Olivia.

Ivy used the fish to play a little air guitar and hopped around the stage, but her foot caught on one of the cables on the floor and she lurched right towards a camera.

Olivia lunged, trying to stop Ivy crashing into it. But it was too late. All Ivy could do was twist at the very last second so that she landed on the fish, rather than on the camera.

'Are you OK?' Olivia asked as she helped Ivy get up.

Ivy nodded, relieved that she didn't break anything – especially the equipment. She straightened her black wrap-around skirt, the good mood disappearing. 'See?' she said, wishing she was anywhere but here. 'Me anywhere near a camera is a disaster waiting to happen.'

Chapter Eight

'**G**irls?' called Mr Vega.

Olivia hadn't heard the door opening, but she turned to see Mr Vega, Lillian and Mr Harker walking into the studio.

'We're over here!' she called.

'But how did you know where we were?' Ivy asked as they drew near.

Harker pushed his wild hair out of his face. 'Big Kev said that he'd seen you coming in here.'

The name definitely suited him, Olivia thought, putting Wacky Walrus carefully back in his place on the display.

'Everything is gravy for this summer's filming,' said Harker. 'You two will be my leading ladies, and Lillian will chaperone, as well as acting as assistant director.'

'And I'll be on set as much as possible,' said Mr Vega, smiling at Lillian.

'So we just need to finish the paperwork.' Harker grinned. 'And you'll both be hugely famous!'

Olivia watched her sister. Ivy had a grimace on her face. *She's only doing it to help me*, Olivia knew. *And it's too much to ask.*

'Actually,' Olivia said, struggling not to cry. 'I don't think we're going to be able to do it after all.' This felt like her greatest acting challenge yet – not to crumple in front of this hotshot producer.

Harker's face fell and Mr Vega looked baffled.

'What are you talking about, man?' Harker said. 'It's all fixed.'

Mr Vega put his back to Harker and asked the girls quietly. 'What's going on? Should we leave?'

'Olivia –' Ivy started, but Olivia didn't want to stop.

'No, it's fine,' Olivia said to both of them. 'Mr Harker, thank you for flying us all out here. I would totally love to be in your movie, but my sister?' Olivia grabbed Ivy's hand. 'My sister would very much like not to be in your movie.'

'*Not* to?' Harker said, like she was speaking a different language.

'Not to,' Ivy confirmed. 'Olivia is the actress – I'm a behind-the-scenes kind of girl.'

There was a moment of silence. 'This is so not cool, man. SO not cool,' Harker murmured, shaking his head.

Deep down, Olivia had known that this moment would come. It had all been too good to be true. 'I'm sorry to put you through this trouble.'

'I thought you girls were on the same wavelength as me.' Harker was pacing up and down, running his hand through his hair. 'I've got a lot of money riding on this. And you were so good in that *Inside Hollywood* interview . . .'

Harker seemed genuinely disappointed.

Olivia sighed. *It just wasn't meant to be*, she thought.

'Well, we're not going to force Ivy into doing something she doesn't want to do,' said Mr Vega. 'Come on, girls.' He started walking to the door.

'Nobody's forcing anyone –' Harker replied and Olivia felt the tension rise.

'Wait a minute,' Ivy said, stopping everyone. 'Let's get together!'

'Huh?' said Harker.

'What do you mean, Ivy?' asked Lillian softly.

'I mean, that song from *The Parent Trap*!' Ivy said. 'The actress in that movie wasn't a twin. She acted both sisters' parts.'

Olivia wasn't sure what Ivy was getting at.

'Why can't Olivia play both parts?' Ivy said to Harker. 'You've already seen her do goth in *The Groves*, and everyone knows that she's perfect for Carmina. Think what a great selling point that will be! One actress, two roles!'

Harker narrowed his eyes and looked at Olivia. 'Can you be a green-screen queen?'

'What does that mean?' Mr Vega asked.

'She'd have to act with herself,' Lillian explained, 'filming half of the conversations in front of a green screen, so they could edit it to look like she was talking to herself.'

'I really want to try,' Olivia said, feeling a flash of hope.

'Dude,' said Harker. 'This could work. It could be my new promotional twist. All those rumours about a second actress . . . we'd trip them out!'

Ivy made her fish do a little happy dance and Olivia wanted to join in.

'We'll set up some test screenings for tomorrow,' Harker said. 'But I'm jazzed, baby!'

He shook Mr Vega's hand, and then Ivy's. Then he pointed at Olivia. 'You go and be a star tonight at the awards. Did I tell you? You're up for the Bright New Star of this year. You just concentrate on that. We'll seal the deal tomorrow.'

Then it hit her – not only had she not lost the part, she'd won a second part, *and* she only had four hours to get ready for the biggest night of her life!

🦇   🦇   🦇

Ivy was seeing stars. She was sitting in a luxurious green room filled with celebrities.

'I can't believe it!' she whispered to Olivia.

She was less than ten feet away from James, Joe and John from the Killer Bees. Joe was twirling his drumsticks in the air and John had a tiny button on his t-shirt that said, 'Buzz off'. It was almost impossible to keep her cool. She'd been texting brags to Brendan ever since the band had walked in.

Today had ended up being a really good day, against all odds.

First, when they'd arrived, Ivy managed to convince Olivia that she really didn't need to walk down the red carpet with her. Jackson had arrived at the show early to prepare for hosting, so Olivia had walked down the red carpet – the skirt of her gorgeous, full-length turquoise dress intact – with Mr Vega and Lillian.

Ivy had snuck behind the crowds to a roped-off area by the entrance. This was for people who didn't want to face the cameras. She flashed her badge and was let into the building, with just enough time to glance down the carpet to

Olivia. Her twin had been turning in her silver heels, looking just like a model. She'd had her hair pinned up in an elegant bun with chandelier earrings and all the photographers had been desperate to get her picture.

By contrast, people could easily have mistaken Ivy for backstage crew. She was wearing a black T-shirt that said Black Hole and black cargo pants.

After they'd met in the lobby, Ivy and Olivia had been shown to the backstage area while the adults headed for the audience. They'd passed a dozen B-list celebs, including the tanned guy from *Shop Hopping* and the dog-training lady from *Barking Mad*.

Now, in the green room, Ivy was perched next to her sister on a black leather sofa with snacks and drinks spread out all over the glass coffee table in front of them. Ivy couldn't stop watching her favourite band.

James looked up and smiled at her.

'Oh, my goodness. James just looked at me!' Ivy scrunched her toes up in excitement. 'Was that a smile? Did he just *smile* at me?'

'Calm down!' Olivia whispered. 'What happened to unimpressed, goth Ivy?'

'Well,' Ivy replied, 'she's staring at the most goth-tastic band alive. It would only be right and proper to get a little weak at the knees.'

Then a group of VIP fans came in, waving autograph books, blocking her view.

'Would it be unprofessional if I throw things at them until they move?' Ivy asked innocently.

'Don't you dare,' Olivia replied. 'I'm nervous enough as it is!'

There were three awards before Olivia was supposed to be ready in case she won the Bright New Star award.

'Whether or not I win, I have to make sure I

keep smiling because the cameras will all be on me,' Olivia said. 'And then if I win, I have to make a speech and introduce the winner of the Brightest Star award!'

'You'll do great ... especially with Jackson right up there next to you.'

Olivia smiled.

'Olivia Abbott?' called an officious-looking woman with a clipboard.

Olivia took a deep breath and stood up.

The woman nodded. 'We need you in the wings by camera six until it's almost time for the nominations to be announced.'

Ivy gave Olivia a hug. 'You are the brightest new star, no matter what. Don't forget, you've got something they don't have.'

'You mean the *Eternal Sunset* role?' Olivia said.

'No ... me!' Ivy grinned.

Olivia laughed. 'You are the best.' She waved

and clicked away in her silver heels.

Ivy looked around the green room. The Killer Bees had disappeared, maybe to get ready to present an award, but Ivy caught sight of Jessica Phelps – wearing a blue dress with Olivia's shark-bite skirt – surrounded by a gaggle of admirers.

Ivy growled under her breath. She knew Jessica was up for the Brightest Star award, and it was almost inevitable that she would get it.

A man with a slicked-back ponytail, all clad in black, bustled through the green room crowd and whispered in Jessica's ear, pressing a small package into her hands.

Jessica's eyes lit up and she dismissed her hangers-on. Ivy's spidey-sense tingled. *She's up to something.*

Jessica slipped through the crowd, flashing smiles left and right. Ivy stood up and discreetly followed as closely as she dared.

She had to duck under a catwalk model shaking out her hair and around a dance group bopping in unison despite there not being any music.

Jessica left the green room and made a bee-line for a bank of monitors and video equipment, where four engineers were busily pushing buttons and shouting cues to each other.

She sidled up to one and caught his attention. Ivy couldn't hear what Jessica was saying, but she could see that the diva was laying on all her charms. The engineer was pushing his glasses back up his nose and leaning closer and closer.

Jessica stood on her tiptoes to whisper into his ear, deliberately putting her hand on his arm.

He seemed to resist her suggestion for a minute but then she took out a pen and wrote something on his hand – probably her phone number. He nodded and Jessica pressed the packet the ponytail man had given her into his hand. The engineer nodded again and Jessica strutted off.

Ivy ducked behind a spare podium and watched the engineer open the packet to find a DVD inside. Jessica had passed him something to play during the awards.

On a nearby monitor, Ivy saw that they were just announcing a tribute to their host, Jackson Caulfield. Ivy narrowed her eyes. Something bad was about to happen. She had to find Olivia.

'Pardon me,' Ivy asked a runner. 'Where is camera six?'

'On the other side.' He pointed and Ivy ran as fast as her chunky books would take her.

🦇　　🦇　　🦇

Olivia had a great view of the stage. Jackson was smiling, cracking little jokes and being his usual charming self.

She was so proud to be his girlfriend. She just wished she didn't have to hide it any more.

'He's doing great,' Amy whispered. She was wearing a gold cowl-neck dress, with her red hair loose over her shoulders.

'He is,' Olivia agreed.

'And now . . .' an announcer's voice boomed over the auditorium speakers, 'a tribute to our wonderful host, Jackson Caulfield!'

The audience went wild and there was a close-up of Jackson at the hosting podium smiling and turning to watch the huge screens behind him.

Instead of Jackson's face, Jessica's face filled the screen.

'What's this?' Amy said. 'This isn't what we approved!' Amy whirled around to the nearest stage hand. 'Who put on this video?'

Olivia watched as Jessica's image filled the screen. 'Hi, Jackson, sweetie!' She blew a kiss at the camera. 'I couldn't let them do any old boring tribute – and we've gotten so close . . .' she paused for emphasis and Olivia wanted to throw something at the screen, 'that I wanted to do something a little special to say thank you for making filming *The Groves* so much fun.'

Olivia glanced over at Jackson at the podium and he looked confused. He caught her eye in the wings and gave a helpless shrug.

Photographs started flashing up on the screen of Jackson and Jessica filming scenes at the Meat and Greet, picnicking in a park and holding hands by a lake. It looked to Olivia more like it was a tribute to them as a couple.

'Don't worry, girls,' Jessica's voice came over the images. 'I'm not taking credit for taming America's most eligible bachelor . . . because someone called Olivia beat me to it!'

Amy gasped and Olivia felt her stomach

twist. She had to take a deep breath to stop from retching. Jackson's mouth was set in a grim line, steeling himself for whatever was coming next.

Then a video clip started of someone clearly filming through a bush. It was Aunt Rebecca's ranch. On the huge screen for everyone to see, Jackson got out of the Daniels' van, rushed over to Olivia, scooped her up and gave her a big kiss.

And, just like that, the secret was out.

Olivia had wanted the world to know, but she didn't want Jackson's fans to find out like this – especially right before she had to face the cameras for the newcomer award.

There was loud booing from the audience.

'Who is that?' one girl shouted.

'Jackson stealer!' called another.

So much for being a star at the awards like Harker

wanted, Olivia thought. *I'm promotional poison!*

The film was still playing out behind her, and there was a glimpse of Ivy on the screen – the first time anyone had seen Ivy and Olivia together in a film.

'They tried to keep that secret from us!' someone cried out. Olivia couldn't believe it. How many more things was she going to get attacked for?

Just then, Ivy burst into the wings. 'Olivia!' she called.

'What is going on?' Amy raged at a stage manager.

He looked terrified and shouted into his headset. 'Commercial break! Go! Now!'

Jackson, still in front of the audience, was forcing a smile but people were up out of their seats, the video had cut out part-way through and the whole event was in chaos.

Olivia couldn't face it any more. She dropped her bag on the nearest chair and fled.

'Olivia!' Ivy called, but Olivia couldn't stop. She had to get away.

Chapter Nine

'Where is she?' Jackson demanded, rushing over to the wings the instant the commercial break began.

'I want somebody FIRED!' Amy was shouting.

'I don't know,' Ivy admitted. 'But we'll find her.'

Ivy took off in the direction that Olivia went, desperately hoping that her sister hadn't left the building. She wished there was something she could have done to prevent this mess.

'Where did she go?' Jackson demanded of a stunned stagehand.

He pointed towards the back of the stage area and Jackson set off after Ivy, with a producer shouting that Jackson had to be back on stage in three minutes.

'Jackson!' Amy called after them.

Ivy rushed up to a woman all in black, carrying a brush and hand-mirror. 'Which way did the girl in turquoise go?'

The make-up artist pointed along the curtain.

Ivy and Jackson tore down the path and eventually found Olivia in a small dressing room tucked away behind a bunch of glittering backdrop props.

Her face was buried in her arms, as she leaned on a counter in front of a well-lit mirror. When Olivia looked up to see who was at the door, Ivy could see that her sister's cheeks were streaked with tears.

Ivy rushed in to hug her, with Jackson right

behind. Ivy felt tears welling in her own eyes seeing her sister so upset.

'I should never have dreamed I could belong here,' Olivia said.

'Oh, Olivia,' Jackson said. 'This is all my fault. I should have made Amy let us go public weeks ago.'

'I'm sorry, too,' Amy said from the doorway. 'I've handled this exactly the wrong way.'

Olivia shook her head. 'It's not even that. It's awful to get booed but, really, I'm just horrified that Jessica could be so vindictive.'

Ivy decided right then and there that something had to be done about Jessica.

'I will never work with her again,' Jackson vowed.

The stage manager knocked sharply on the door. 'There's no time for this. Jackson you're on.'

'Give me a minute!' Jackson insisted. 'Olivia,

please don't leave. Don't give up.'

'There's no way Harker will want me now,' Olivia said.

'Jackson –' the stage manager started again.

'Can it!' Amy cut him off. The man's mouth fell open in shock. 'This mess is your crew's fault. How could you have let that video get played? You will just have to deal for a little longer.'

Ivy was impressed. Amy really had Jackson's best interests at heart.

Jackson knelt down beside Olivia.

'You should go,' Olivia told him.

'I'm not going anywhere until I know you're all right,' he said gently.

Ivy could see that it was making things worse for Olivia to be ruining Jackson's evening. 'I'm here,' she said. 'I'll make sure Olivia's OK.'

Jackson hesitated.

'Really,' Olivia said. 'Go.'

Jackson got to his feet and turned. The stage manager looked about to weep with relief. He started gabbling into his walkie-talkie, 'We are go!' and he practically dragged Jackson away.

In the moment of silence, Amy emptied her little bag out on to the counter. Make-up remover, tissues, mascara, lipstick and blusher clattered on to the laminate surface.

'What happens next is entirely up to you, sweetie,' she said quietly. 'Whatever you choose won't be easy, but it's my job to give you the tools you need, if you decide to stay.'

'Thank you, Amy,' Olivia said, sniffling. 'You're a good friend.'

Ivy was still clutching Olivia's handbag when it started chirping. Olivia shook her head, and Ivy knew her sister didn't want to deal with it right now.

'You take care of it,' Olivia said.

There were already three text messages. One was from their dad, so Ivy quickly texted him their location and to say things were OK. The next was from Camilla, so Ivy sent another reassuring note, but the third was from Charlotte Brown.

Ivy frowned. *Oh no, she didn't!* Ivy guessed that Charlotte couldn't resist the chance to gloat. But when she opened the text, it was a link to a video with a short message from Charlotte: 'That was so un-cool. Get her back.'

Ivy stepped out of the dressing room to watch the video. What she saw made her gasp and then smile.

The truth is out there, Ivy thought. *Justice can be done.*

She popped her head into Olivia's dressing room. 'I'll be right back.'

Ivy headed straight to the bank of monitors,

and to the engineer who was about to lose his job, if Amy had anything to do with it.

'Hey.' She pointed at him and hoped her face showed that he was in no position to refuse. 'I've got a deal for you . . .'

Olivia looked at herself in the mirror.

She was alone, for the moment. Ivy had rushed off and Amy had gone to give her some space. Her face was streaked with mascara tears and her hair stuck out in all directions from her bun.

She looked as though she'd just starred in some action movie, not as if she was lined up to appear in a glamorous awards show.

'Can I do this?' she said to herself.

She had two choices: stay and face the booing crowds, or go back home and live quietly, without all the pressure.

She took Amy's make-up remover and started wiping away her ruined eye shadow. As she worked, she remembered what it felt like when Harker had first chosen her for *Eternal Sunset*. It was the best feeling. And getting interviewed by Chuck was one of the highlights of her year. Singing 'Wacky Walrus' with Ivy in that studio felt like she'd come home.

But every time she saw Jessica with Jackson, it felt miserable. The premiere when she couldn't walk in with Jackson, and being spied on by paparazzi – all of those things were less than perfect.

'It's just not worth it,' Olivia said out loud.

It didn't matter whether or not the world knew about her relationship. She understood what she and Jackson were all about. She could go back home to Franklin Grove and be happy. She had cheerleading; she had her friends and she still had the best boyfriend in the world.

'I'm lucky, really,' she murmured. She could feel determination rising up inside her. Why should she run away like a coward when she knew she had so many things to be proud of?

'One last night,' she decided. She wasn't going to walk out on her role at the awards – she had commitments. She'd do what she had to, show a brave face – and then leave it all behind without any regrets.

No vampire diva actress was going to scare her away. Olivia might not have to file her fangs, but she could put up a fight any vampire would be proud of.

She inspected the make-up scattered across the counter, then picked out Amy's mascara like it was a weapon.

'Now or never,' she told herself, leaning towards the mirror and reapplying her make-up.

'No one puts Olivia in the corner.'

It was time to show the world what she was made of.

🦇   🦇   🦇

'Where is my daughter?'

Ivy heard her dad's grave voice booming across the vast backstage area. He was berating some poor technician, with Lillian trying to talk him down, so Ivy hurried over.

'Dad!' she called. 'She's over here.'

'There is no way my daughter will be treated like this by anyone,' Mr Vega declared as he pushed his way through a troupe of dancers.

'She's OK, really, Dad,' Ivy said. 'Come on. I'll take you to her.'

When they got to the dressing room, Olivia had fixed her make-up and taken her hair down. The style was a bit tousled, but Olivia could definitely pull off the casual-chic look.

'What a transformation!' Ivy said.

'Don't sound so surprised,' Olivia said, laughing and hugging Mr Vega. 'I'm ready to get back out there and smile.'

'Well done,' Mr Vega replied. 'Good for you.'

'Are you sure you're OK?' Lillian asked. 'That must have been awful.'

Olivia nodded. 'It was, but I'm over it now.'

'You know,' Lillian went on, 'Jessica is not representative of the whole of the film industry. There are good people here, too.'

'I know that's true,' Mr Vega said, looking right at Lillian, who immediately blushed.

Ivy gave Olivia a pointed look. If that wasn't proof of something going on between the two of them, what more did Olivia need?

Mr Vega cleared his throat. 'Uh, girls, I have something to tell you.'

'Oh, please!' Ivy interrupted. 'I've seen this

romance coming from a mile off.'

'You have?' Lillian asked.

'The dinners, the blushing,' Ivy replied. 'I'm really happy for you both.'

Mr Vega looked at Olivia. 'I know there's a lot on your plate at the minute, but –'

'But nothing,' Olivia said. 'I'm delighted.' She gave Lillian a big hug. 'If I hadn't been so wrapped up in myself these past few days, I would have seen it coming, too.'

'You've had a lot to take in,' Mr Vega said.

'But this is the end,' Olivia said. 'I'm not interested in all the craziness. After tonight, I'm going back to Franklin Grove, just little old me.'

'No way!' Ivy said. 'You're not giving up on your dream!'

'But in my dream, it's fun and happy and nice,' Olivia said. 'All this other stuff just isn't me.'

Ivy frowned. Jessica was getting just what

she wanted — her new competition was giving up. 'Ignore Jessica. What about the nomination? Regardless of Jackson, people liked you enough to think you were one of the top five Brightest New Stars.'

Olivia paused. 'Yes, but . . .'

'Just wait and see,' Ivy insisted. 'Don't make your final decision yet.'

Lillian put a hand on Olivia's arm. 'You're a born actress, Olivia. You should at least wait and see how the award goes. Take it from me — I know talent when I see it.'

'It might be a tough audience,' Mr Vega said, 'but only leave if you want to, Olivia. Don't let anyone else make that decision for you.'

'Olivia Abbott?' called a stage manager. 'We need you now. Jackson's waiting.'

Olivia looked around from Ivy, to Lillian, to Mr Vega. 'We'll just have to see.'

Ivy just knew that her sister would charm them all, if she could get out there and talk to everyone. Ivy hoped with all her heart that Olivia would win the award.

'Good luck,' Ivy whispered.

Olivia strode out of the room and Ivy crossed her fingers, hoping that the world would just give her sister a chance.

Chapter Ten

O livia slipped on to the red velvet seat beside Mr Vega. During a video after the commercial break, she'd been escorted out into the audience so that the cameras could see her reaction as the award was announced. Almost immediately, a cameraman closed in, his huge black camera lens pointed right at her.

Jackson stood at the podium and smiled at the audience. He didn't show any of the stress that Olivia guessed he might be feeling. The last thing he'd had to deal with before going on stage was her being upset. 'And now, I am delighted to announce the nominees for the Brightest New Star award, given to a debut actor or actress with a bright future in Hollywood.'

Olivia knew she had about ten seconds before her face was splashed across the huge screen in the auditorium and broadcast live to the nation – they always showed the faces of all the nominees as the award was being announced. She ignored the panicky feeling that was welling up in her and focused on one moment: it was just after Christmas. Ivy, Mr Vega and her parents were sitting together in the Abbott's kitchen. All the crazy family together.

That's what matters in all of this, Olivia thought to herself.

Jackson called out clearly, 'Olivia Abbott . . .'

There was an awkward silence, then a smattering of polite applause. Everyone in the audience was in full formal wear. One old lady was wearing a tiara and the man next to her was wearing a full tuxedo.

Olivia just kept thinking about her family, to distract herself. Out of the corner of her eye, she could see her big face on the screen.

Jackson read out the other four nominees, whose applause was clearly more than polite. *It's almost over, it's almost over*, Olivia kept telling herself.

'And the winner is . . .'

Olivia felt her heart thumping through her body.

It would be amazing to win, but it was next to impossible. She knew the votes would have been cast long before Jessica's video stunt; there was no way she could have made that big an impact with just one small role in a Jackson Caulfield flick.

But a little voice inside her said, 'It was big

enough to land the *Eternal Sunset* role!'

It was like slow motion as Jackson opened the gold envelope and then looked her way. He locked eyes with her and read out, 'Olivia Abbott!'

There was a loud whooping noise – that sounded distinctly like a certain sister of hers – and then an awkward hush descended on the audience.

Mr Vega squeezed Olivia's hand. 'Go on,' he told her. 'Enjoy your moment.'

Olivia stepped out into the aisle and walked up on to the stage, squinting under the glare of the lights.

'Congratulations, Olivia,' Jackson said, leaning into the microphone, as Olivia strode towards his podium.

Now she could see that the huge auditorium was packed. There were hundreds of people staring at her. Young girls were scattered through the rows – clearly Jackson fans, judging by their scowls. One of them, wearing pink taffeta, stuck her tongue out at Olivia.

Jackson handed her a tall glass trophy and the envelope. She glanced down to see that it really was her name written there.

She stepped in front of the microphone and said, 'I'm so surprised, but happy.' Jackson gave her a huge, proud smile and Olivia knew that this might be her only chance to set the record straight about her and Jackson.

'I know some of you might be disappointed by the video that you saw earlier – believe me, that took me by surprise. But so did falling for this wonderful person.

'At the beginning of the year, I was a nobody – just a Jackson fan standing at the barriers when a film set in my home town was being shot. Then, in a blur, I had a role in a movie and a mega-famous boyfriend. It was totally over-whelming, but the best feeling ever.'

She smiled at Jackson and there were a few faint sounds of 'ooh' and 'ah' from the audience. The pink taffeta girl was grinning now. 'We never meant to mislead anyone, but it was all so new that we didn't want any more pressure on our relationship.'

She stopped, not sure if there was anything else to say.

In the pause, someone called out, 'We love you, Olivia and Jackson!' The old lady with the tiara clapped and nodded while the girl in pink whooped and cheered.

Next to her, Jackson applauded and winked.

'Thank you so much for this award,' Olivia said. She saw Harker standing in the wings giving her a thumbs up. 'There's just one more thing I have to say. A big "thank you" to my sister, Ivy.

We are complete opposites, but she is the best person I know, and more people should be like her. Without Ivy, I wouldn't be here today. We all need family, right?'

The auditorium exploded in applause, and Olivia felt so much better. Jackson scooped her up in a huge hug, which just made the audience cheer even louder.

When the noise settled, Jackson whispered in Olivia's ear. 'You have to announce the next award.'

Olivia nodded.

He pressed an envelope into her hands.

Olivia looked out at the audience, which had more welcoming faces now, and said, 'I'm honoured to be able to present the next award: the Brightest Star award.' The nominees were all written on the back of the envelope. 'The nominees are: Beverly Bonds, Naomi Coleman, George Morrow . . .' She had to take a deep breath before saying the next name, 'Jessica Phelps, Mark Richter and Emily Tipman.'

As she fumbled with opening the envelope, a hush fell over the audience. She could see Harker watching from the side of the stage.

This was the biggest award of the night, and Olivia felt sure about who was going to win. She pulled the little card out of the envelope to confirm it.

'Jessica Phelps,' she read out and the audience burst into even louder applause.

Blonde hair flowing, Jessica floated out on to the stage. She'd changed her outfit and was wearing a long red dress with diamond studs and an amazing diamond choker. She looked classy.

Too bad she is everything but classy, Olivia thought. But she smiled and clapped along with everyone else. Jackson handed Jessica a trophy, and over his shoulder, Jessica gave Olivia a pointed look.

Jackson broke away and leaned over to the microphone. 'Before we hear from our winner, let's watch her tribute video.'

He kept clapping and turned to watch the big screen. A familiar face appeared.

'Hi, I'm Charlotte Brown. You don't know me – yet – but I've got a secret to share with you.'

Olivia was stunned. She looked at Jackson, but he seemed just as confused.

'I have a special tribute video to show you about my new friend Jessica. I want people to know the truth about your favourite movie star.'

Charlotte's face disappeared and a grainy shot appeared of Jessica in the Meat and Greet. It was obviously filmed on someone's camera phone.

Olivia snuck a glance at Jessica, who was beginning to look concerned.

Jessica's voice rang out clearly, thanking a fan.

'You guys are the reason that I do what I

do, and I love you all!' She gave the slightly overweight girl a hug.

'I heard you were going to star in the movie of *Eternal Sunset*,' said the girl.

'Oh, I would be honoured just to audition for that role,' Jessica said sweetly.

The girl beamed.

'My friend is filming this, so I can put this meeting up on my fan site – if that's OK with you,' said Jessica.

The girl nodded, looking ecstatic, and scurried away.

In the auditorium, the audience clapped, but the video didn't stop there.

As the fan walked away Jessica turned to the camera and her smile changed into a grimace. 'These stupid fans are just so obsessive,' she said. 'And did you see what she was wearing?'

On stage, Jessica was turning white and

shaking her head, backing away.

'Ugh,' Jessica on the screen sneered. 'And do you know what? I hate those stupid books like *Eternal Sunset*. They are so lame.'

There was a stony silence from the audience.

'Loser fans are the very worst part of being a mega-star.' Jessica tossed her hair and sat back down in the booth.

The real-life Jessica whirled around, mouth hanging open. 'I . . . I . . . I . . .' For once she seemed unable to speak.

Olivia remembered overhearing how mean Jessica was to Charlotte in the Meat and Greet the last time she saw the two of them together. Jessica might be one of the most famous, talented and powerful young actresses in Hollywood, but that didn't mean she could cross Charlotte Brown and not suffer some cheerleader revenge.

Olivia looked at Jackson. He nodded towards the wings. 'Go on, get out of here,' he whispered. 'You shouldn't have to be part of this.' Olivia hurried offstage, just as the massive boos started to ring out from the crowd . . .

🦇   🦇   🦇

In front of a set of monitors in the green room, with Mr Vega on one side and Lillian on the other, Ivy did a happy dance.

'I will be nice to Charlotte Brown for the rest of my life!' Ivy declared, but then she realised what she had just said. 'Correction: I will *try* to be nice to Charlotte Brown.'

Olivia peeked through the green-room door and lit up when she saw her family there. 'What was that?' she asked, but Ivy didn't want to dish the dirt about how Jessica went all out to swap Olivia's video. It was enough that justice had been done and Jessica had exposed herself.

'Let's just say that we might owe Charlotte a few Beauty Boosting Blueberry smoothies when we get back to Franklin Grove,' Ivy replied. 'As long as I don't have to drink them with her.'

Mr Vega gave Olivia a hug. 'I'm so proud of you, Olivia. First winning the award and then being so mature in the face of all that silliness.'

Lillian smiled. 'And you looked beautiful.'

Jackson burst into the room. 'Olivia!' he cried, rushing over. 'Wow!' He gave Olivia a big hug. 'You were amazing!'

'Thanks,' Olivia whispered.

Harker appeared behind them. 'Dude,' he said to Olivia, shaking his head. 'That was rough, but you really pulled it off. True star quality. How about doing it all over again next year?'

Ivy held her breath. This was Harker asking if Olivia was going to stick with being an actress.

Olivia smiled. 'If we can do it without all

the drama, I would love to be back here again next year.'

Lillian clapped and Mr Vega beamed and Jackson whooped so loud that the other guests in the green room stared. Even Ivy had to admit she was happy for her sister, but there was something that worried her. Did that mean Olivia was going to leave Franklin Grove?

Harker grabbed Olivia's hand to shake it. 'I will definitely be calling your dad tomorrow and we'll make you a Beverly Hills local in no time.' Then he turned to Ivy. 'Are you sure you don't want a shiny award like your sister?' Harker asked. 'We could come up with a new category. The Darkest Star award . . .'

'Tempting,' Ivy replied. 'But this town doesn't exactly go with my colour scheme. And I'm desperate to get back to a certain someone in Franklin Grove.' Ivy wasn't used to being without

Brendan this much and she didn't want to be.

Harker shrugged. 'I might have known; there is always some boy. Check you later, then,' he said and sauntered off.

'So,' Ivy said to Olivia, not sure if she wanted to hear the answer. 'What are you thinking? Are you going to move out here to Beverly Hills?'

If her sister wanted to follow her dream, Ivy wouldn't stop her.

Olivia shook her head. 'No way. I've only just moved to Franklin Grove.'

'Me, too!' Jackson put in. 'And I don't want to pack up all those boxes again.'

'Like Jackson's already said, we'll make Hollywood come to us,' Olivia declared. 'Or we can travel for shoots.'

Ivy hugged Olivia again. 'That's the best news I've heard tonight.'

Two hours later, the show had been over for ages and Olivia had been stuffing her face. The green room had been rearranged into a buffet area with sit-down tables and while most of the celebs had gone off to after-show parties, there were still some people hanging around to enjoy the hospitality – and avoid the crowds waiting outside.

'Live television makes me hungry,' Olivia said, with a mouthful of fruit salad.

'Me too,' said Jackson, who had gobbled down two veggie burgers heaped with ketchup. There were plenty of carnivorous options for the fanged members of her family.

Olivia couldn't believe how it had all turned out: a part in a huge movie next to her boyfriend, the approval of fans about her relationship, and her dad had a new potential love in his life.

She looked at Lillian and her bio-dad

fighting over the last bite of chocolate cake. He seemed so happy and Olivia knew that Lillian was great.

Olivia shared a look with Ivy. Her sister was clearly thinking the same thing.

'OK, love birds,' Ivy said. 'Can't we go back to our over-the-top suite for a good night's sleep now?'

Mr Vega stood up. 'You won't hear me arguing. This father-of-the-star act is exhausting.'

Olivia nudged him with her elbow. 'Stop it.' She picked up her award off the table and smiled at it. It felt good to have something to hold on to.

'Thanks!' Olivia called to the production assistant who was helping clear up the buffet table. 'Bye!'

Ivy waved goodbye as well.

'I think there's a side entrance over this way.' Lillian led them out of the green room and past props people breaking down the awards show set.

'After a night like tonight, I'm glad we can just sneak away,' Olivia said. 'I have a feeling things are going to get a little crazier for a while.'

'Not too crazy,' Ivy said, as they approached the side exit. 'There will be no paparazzi stalkers, or they will have me to deal with.'

'Well, if you're my bodyguard —' but Olivia didn't get the chance to finish her sentence.

Lillian had pushed open the door and Olivia's ears were filled with the screaming of a hoard of fans.

'Uh oh,' said Jackson. 'Looks like people didn't want to go home.'

Olivia grinned. 'They must have been waiting for their host!'

'Let's go somewhere else,' Ivy said. Jackson shook his head.

'It's not a red carpet,' he said to Olivia. 'But I've been waiting so long just to walk somewhere with you. Can this be it?'

Olivia beamed. She looked at her dad and Lillian, who smiled encouragingly. 'We'll wait here,' said Mr Vega.

'How can I say no?' Olivia replied. She let Jackson lead her out into the crowd. The noise was overwhelming.

Jackson waved and Olivia followed his lead, raising her hand above her head.

'I don't think they are here for me,' he shouted.

Olivia listened and heard, 'O-liv-i-a! O-liv-i-a!' chanted over and over again. She couldn't believe it.

A young girl holding her mom's hand was waving an autograph book. 'I love your hair!' she shouted.

Olivia stepped over and knelt down as much

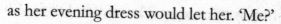

as her evening dress would let her. 'Me?'

'Ohmigosh, yes!' the girl squealed. As Olivia scribbled her name, the little girl said, 'I'm going to be just like you when I grow up.'

Olivia smiled and wrote, 'Be true to yourself,' below her signature.

She and Jackson started signing autographs together and talking to the fans who had waited so long to see them.

Suddenly, the crowd went silent. Jessica had appeared at the exit. Someone booed and then the rest of the crowd joined in.

'Whatever!' Jessica declared and waved her hand dismissively. She clicked away and ducked into the back of a limo.

Olivia couldn't help feeling relieved to see the back of Jessica.

'I hope that's the last we see of her,' Ivy said, linking her arm through Olivia's.

With her sister on one side and her boyfriend on the other — and crowds screaming her name — Olivia couldn't keep the grin off her face. She twirled round on the spot, taking it all in. Remembering the poses that Spencer had taught her, she allowed the photographers to snap her with her new hairstyle.

Everything was going to work out. She could just feel it. With Ivy encouraging her and Jackson on her arm, Olivia knew she could do more and more as an actress. It wasn't just about the dresses or the hype, the crowds of fans or the glamorous hotels. It was about being true to herself.

I did it. I really did it, she thought.

'Happy?' Jackson asked, as she rested her head on his shoulder.

'I couldn't be happier,' she murmured. 'I'm with you, aren't I?'

Jackson leaned over and kissed the tip of

her nose. The crowd exploded into cheers and applause. Jackson brought one arm around Olivia's waist and dipped at the knees to scoop his other arm beneath her legs. Before she knew it, he'd picked her up and was swirling her around and around. She threw her arms around his neck and burst out laughing. She could see the blurry outlines of Ivy, her dad and Lillian all grinning as they watched.

'This is the best moment of my life!' she cried. And she knew this was only the beginning.

Sink your teeth into this!

Being a new girl sucks. But then Olivia Abbott meets her long-lost twin sister, Ivy. They're as different as day and night – and Ivy has a grave secret. But it won't stop them getting to know each other's worlds. After all, blood is thicker than water – and it's certainly tastier!

MY
SISTER THE VAMPIRE

FANGTASTIC!

Sienna Mercer

Sink your teeth into the third book starring Olivia and Ivy

MY SISTER THE VAMPIRE

REVAMPED!

Sienna Mercer

The secret is out – Olivia and Ivy are twins! But some
people are turning in their coffins about it. Ivy's adoptive
dad doesn't believe Olivia won't betray the Franklin
Grove vampires. To prove she can be trusted, Olivia must
pass three tests – but not just any old tests. These are
challenges to really get the blood pumping!

MY SISTER THE VAMPIRE

VAMPALICIOUS

Sienna Mercer

Ivy and Olivia have only been reunited for a few months
and already they can't imagine life without each other.
But Ivy's dad is moving to Europe – taking Ivy with
him! Olivia and Ivy need to change his mind, but will the
skills of two crafty twins be enough to stop a vampire
from spreading his wings?

Sink your teeth into the fifth book starring Olivia and Ivy

Hollywood has come to Franklin Grove!
And while Olivia is getting to know the hot
teen movie star Jackson Caulfield, Ivy is doing
some snooping about. It looks like someone on
the set has a grave secret. Could her twin be
falling for a vampire?

Sink your teeth into the sixth book starring Olivia and Ivy

The twins are in Transylvania, to meet their vampire family. Olivia is nervous – there's a lot at stake. But a smooth-talking boy is immediately taken with her. Ivy can't believe it – it's nearly Valentine's Day and her twin is spending time with a vampire prince!

Sink your teeth into the seventh book starring Olivia and Ivy

Ivy has scared off their long-lost aunt's horse, Lucky. While Olivia is going to have her first kiss with a vampire – not her boyfriend – in the school play! But that's not all... The twins are in a tomb-load of trouble. Could their bio-mom's diary shed some light in the darkness?

EGMONT PRESS: ETHICAL PUBLISHING

Egmont Press is about turning writers into successful authors and children into passionate readers – producing books that enrich and entertain. As a responsible children's publisher, we go even further, considering the world in which our consumers are growing up.

Safety First
Naturally, all of our books meet legal safety requirements. But we go further than this; every book with play value is tested to the highest standards – if it fails, it's back to the drawing-board.

Made Fairly
We are working to ensure that the workers involved in our supply chain – the people that make our books – are treated with fairness and respect.

Responsible Forestry
We are committed to ensuring all our papers come from environmentally and socially responsible forest sources.

For more information, please visit our website at www.egmont.co.uk/ethical

Egmont is passionate about helping to preserve the world's remaining ancient forests. We only use paper from legal and sustainable forest sources, so we know where every single tree comes from that goes into every paper that makes up every book.

This book is made from paper certified by the Forestry Stewardship Council (FSC), an organisation dedicated to promoting responsible management of forest resources. For more information on the FSC, please visit **www.fsc.org**. To learn more about Egmont's sustainable paper policy, please visit **www.egmont.co.uk/ethical**.